T0374446

SHADOWS

SHADOWS

STANLEY J. SERXNER

iUniverse

SHADOWS

iUniverse books may be ordered through booksellers or by contacting:

iUniverse
1663 Liberty Drive
Bloomington, IN 47403
www.iuniverse.com
1-800-Authors (1-800-288-4677)

ISBN: 978-1-5320-8655-7 (sc)
ISBN: 978-1-5320-8656-4 (e)

Print information available on the last page.

iUniverse rev. date: 11/12/2019

CONTENTS

ACKNOWLEDGEMENTS

ART by Bobby Iadiccicco

Thanks, A. and H. D. for the use of their names.

Much appreciated words and thoughts from
Joyce, my senior-editor-in-chief

The folks at iUniverse for technical support

SHADOWS

Our war, my buddy's and mine, is restricted to our two man foxhole and a 360º field of fire. We try not to shoot each other. Our home away from home is complete with sleeping section, grenade sump and overhead cover in case of nosy, noisy neighbors and other bad type vibrations. The rest of our weaponry and location is classified, so I'm told.

We are proud to say, my buddy and I – when my buddy is in the mood for conversation – that we hewed our hole out of refractory and unforgiving alien soil strictly according to military specifications as described and depicted in FM (Field Manual) 21-7, "Combat Training of the Individual Soldier and Patrolling". Copies of this and other FM's mentioned herein may be obtained free of charge – as long as supplies last – by sending a stamped, self-destructing mailing container to:

> Senior Sergeants Doe and Roe
> Two Assholes in a Foxhole
> APO 666
> Seattle, Washington 98765

San Francisco and surrounding areas, our previous Army Post Office, was urged into the Pacific Ocean some time ago by Forces which augmented those of Mother Nature, i.e., a nuclear boost to the San Andreas Fault supplied the augmentation.

So, here we sit, dipped in ennui. Masters of our own universe, maybe of our own war, considering that we really do not know what is happening in the sectors around us.

An occasional overhead whistle – incoming - outgoing? Communications have been less than perfect.* So bad that static seems to make perfect sense. I suspect that THEY are having the same problems. Who are THEY? Damned if I know. Allies and enemies seem to shift allegiances every time my foxhole mate and I hear a WHOOSH or HSOOHW overhead.

All I know is we haven't been PUKED yet. PUKED? Let me explain. I will articulate as distinctly as I can through the voicemitter of my latest model M17A1 Field Protective mask, the care, maintenance and manipulation of which is found in FM 21-15, "Care and Use of Individual Clothing and Equipment" and FM-41, "Individual Defense NBC (Nuclear, Biological and Chemical), which also may be obtained by … where was I? Ah, PUKED.

The origin of that trenchant syllable is in the phrase, "PUKE 'EM, DON'T NUKE 'EM!" Remember also the "Nuke 'Em 'Til They Glow" enthusiasts? Remember the anti-nuke crowd?

You do? May Aeolus, God of the Jetstream, blow upon you.

Well, the anti-nukers finally got their point across to the political-military circle jerkers through sheer logic and compromise. The disappearance of San Francisco helped. The anti-nukers opined that throwing around nukes got rid of EVERTHING! Nothing would be left for the "victor" or "vanquished". Not to mention centuries of non-habitation!

Whereas, by careful application of Biological and Chemical warfare, the inhabitants of the desired territory would sicken, PUKE and die off, leaving the real estate intact for subsequent occupation, which was the whole point of the exercise, yes?

It is to be hoped that the "victorious" occupier had all his bugs in a row, with antidotes and antibodies for his troops and my body lies over the ocean … oops. Excuse me. Mind wandered. Then the real estate agents take over, enslaving what remained of the original inhabitants, if any and raise their flag.

What splendid, moving logic, the anti-nukers. Let's hear it for the buggers! Except for tracts of California, very few nuclear weapons were then used - "low-yield" - Now, that's a compromise!

So, "PUKE 'EM, DON'T NUKE 'EM" won the day and the night and made useless fortunes for the bug-makers of the world. Perish and putrefy. The order of the day (and night). See FM 212-10/AFM 161-10 "Field Hygiene and Sanitation" for further information. Gentle listener, you might also wish to peruse FM 21-76, "Survival and Escape". The Army has an FM for everything.

Well – so, here we sit, my buddy and I, tightly taut, hanging loosely, dipped in ant-neo-bug crappola. But I am not bugged. It hasn't affected me affected me affected me sorry. Slip of the lip.

I remem mem mem ber echoes and shadows of the old ecosystem when thee and I were young and green dear, upon the green, green grass, not from the green, green gas. Sigh!

So, here we sit, my buddy and I, in our MOPP gear (Mission Oriented Protective Posture), and big damn coverover homogenized mask and hood and gloves and boots with so many variations and combinations for better survival that it gladdens the heart, lungs and mind The whole nine yards, as some ant-metric wit quipped. One is isolated/insulated/captivated – all alone by the telephone – forgive me, I wander again. Who gives a shit?

Ever try to shit out of a Chemical Protective Overgarment? It ain't easy exposing one's blind cheeks to the jolliest poisons invented by the febrile fecal gray cells of man and then mutated just for the hell of it? Even if an area for 'proper disposal of waste' is a part of one's personal home-away-from-home architecture. Gives one a case of the ass, buddy.

How's it going, ol' buddy and foxhole mate? Still incommunicado, hey, Señor?

Thus, we continue to PUKE whomever is left. Even their shadows. No nuclear glow. Putrescent luminescence. Whomever is left. Subjunctive in Spanish. "Quienquiera que se quede." I picked up a little Spanish on a SpecOps once upon a time. Ooops. Now I'll have to kill you!!

Ah, who is ally – who is enemy? Who still knows? Who can care? WHO CARES? Tough on civilians, though – men, women, children, husbands, wives. Lovers. Adam and Eve and Lillith. But I remem mem mem ber. Yes, I do. The beginning and the end. Alpha and Omega. Aleph and Tav. All of it.

Except for one year. One year. I'd give you the DTG (Date Time Group) on DD Form 173/2 Joint Message Form, BUT I DON'T REMEMMEMMEMBER!! that one year.

Shock induced trauma? Did it happen when the rumors about the Grand Puking were substantiated – that year of the shadows when the world became shadows?

Female shadows. The shadow shape of her breasts, her buttocks, against the clinging material of her raiment. It's not raiming raim, you know, it's raiming sweet violence. The summer shadows on the shadow of her body. The summer of our discovery of each other. The summer of our discontent. Did our shadows mingle? Conjoin? Did they? The swell of her breasts.... I wander again.

Listen, Senior Sergeants Doe and Roe. Can we find ourselves in the Song of Songs, Shir HaShirim, which is the Song of Solomon in hill and shadows? And the green green gas? Clouds of it.

Shadows … once, in a repple depple – replacement depot – standing outside my squad tent amidst an accidental silence,

I watched the day purple into night over the jagged, deep shadows ringing the valley. For a long, long instant I stood entranced; sky and mountains were of the same color. One thin, jagged black line differentiated them, drawn across my sight. Then all went black. Tomorrow stood in the wings. The wings of the Angel of Death. HaMalach HaMa'avet.

Back to the MLR (Main Line of Resistance). With the Angel de la Muerte WOOSHing and HSOOWing overhead.

In my naïve wisdom. Sitting here, rifle carefully propped up against the foxhole walls (FM 23-5, U.S, Caliber .30, M1) I've wondered more than once why shadows obscured that year of my life.

Was it a trauma? Learning that where shadows are now there once had been substance? My being of bright-eyed flesh and blood once? Was there ever the unclouded joy of first discovery? Had I been married? Did I have a girlfriend? Wife and girlfriend? Cinnamon eyes? Seablue eyes? Obsidian eyes? Redhead? Brunette? Short? Tall? Zaftig? A million other qualities, attributes ....

The shadows blurred; my beloveds? Was I beloved? There's no way of knowing what another person feels. Ninety-nine percent of one's loves, hates, fears cannot be communicated. Every man and woman in the world is locked inside him/herself from birth to death. Is there no true communion between people? Touch? Ah – untouchable shadows. Lord of Shadows. Señor de las Sombras. Do you exist? Should I worship you as my mind grows cloudier? Joyous clouds of bugs and mists and death. Shadows of shadows.

Here we sit, dipped in sweat no matter the season of our war. Two assholes in a foxhole. Sitting on our dead asses. I think that my buddy is dead. A soldier carved in stone MOPP gear. Or stoned? We were at one time supplied with certain performance-enhancing substances for obvious reasons until the supply and the providers - ah — how to say this? - were no longer in a position to continue to supply us. Who cares?

Who cares? I do. I will attend to my stoned stone cold dead buddy in accordance with AR (Army Regulation) 670-1, "Wear and Appearance of Army Iniforms and Insignia" and bury him honorably in our two-man home away from home. Where else?

The truth, the antiseptic truth: the shadows are pigments of my chlorophyll imagination, recalling the green green grass. Green eyes! She has green eyes! Existenceless. False mountains, hills, curves, breasts. All that is real is my stone cold dead buddy and my rifle and my MOPP gear and ….

So here we sit, dipped in brainwash, awash in chemicals and biologicals and illogicals. And crappola.

Dipped in shadows. Jaggy raggy curved shadows. Fuck 'em. I'm gonna sit here dipped in death for the rest of my natural life.

*Refer to FMs 21-75 and 24-18, Communications.

THE MINYAN

My name is Monica Kelly. I am 18 years old, just graduated in June, 2018 from St. Cecilia's Catholic High in Waltham, Mass. I'm blonde, blue eyed, 5"6" and called pretty by my boyfriend Patrick Callahan, who is 20, six feet even, brown hair, blue eyes and my parents really like him. I have a younger sister 13, and an older brother, 21. They are OK.

We studied a bit about the Holocaust in our European history class, with WWII. The nuns told us WWII was pretty bad for the Jews. About six million of them and a million more Roma, or Gypsies and other people that the Nazis didn't like died in concentration camps. It was bad for the Catholics, too.

My parents didn't know much more about the Holocaust and told me not to get into it. I never met a survivor. I guess I met some Jews, though.

But for some reason, I don't know why, it became like I spent more and more time studying about it. My parents and Patrick told me to stop worrying about something past and gone. But I felt like a compulsion to keep investigating.

"It's going to ruin your whole summer, you keep it up", Mom and Dad said together.

"No, it won't, just a couple of hours a day", I insisted.

Patrick thought it was past history and had been studied to death, he said, no pun intended.

But I couldn't stop. I finally came up with the idea of actually visiting a concentration camp.

When I said that I wanted to go see one, my parents had a fit - one big fat fit apiece.

"Oh no you're not", both screamed at the same time. "it's a bunch of dead Jews," and more.

I'm not going to go into the verbal battle. Nasty harsh words were not exchanged, but dire threats were made, none of which I will elaborate. My sister and brother both thought that it was a great adventure but kept on the side lines.

Finally, I told them that going on a visit would get the whole thing out of my system. I had saved enough from my allowance to get a coach ticket on LOT, the Polish airline. I even contacted a tour group so as not to be alone.

The one proviso was that Patrick accompany me; my parents would pay and pray for both of us - first class, yet, in the hope that a smooth and comfortable trip would be it, with a capital IT. I could use my allowance for some souvenirs, maybe, and get back to being Monica, their daughter.

Patrick and I are going to Auschwitz-Birkenau, which is in Poland and is famous, if that's the word, for a big sign over the entrance gate. There are lots of concentration camps, I know.

So we flew first class from New York, landed in Kracow and met the rest of the tour group, twenty people, in the Hotel Monika. Patrick had a room with another single guy and I roomed with a single lady. The hotel staff thought that it was funny that my name was Monica and sort of treated me well. The Hotel was about 50 Km from the camp. It had a Polish name too "Osweicim". Got a funny name in Yiddish, "Oshpitzin", like. one of he Jewish people, on the tour told me. The Jews I met on the tour are regular people. I found out that Yiddish was a language that Jews talked.

We really toured the area, It was very sad.

"Let's go again tomorrow, because I'm going to stay overnight in one of the barracks," I said casually to Patrick.

It took a minute for him to digest. "WHAT?" he yelled. It was a good thing that we were in a sort of alone place in the area. "YOU ARE GOING TO DO WHAT? ARE YOU PLAIN NUTS!! CRAZY. I didn't hear you right, did I" he looked me square in the eye.

"Yes, Patrick, you heard me right and I'm glad that you didn't ask me to repeat what I just said."

"For God's sake", he gritted out in lower case, "Why, in HeavEN'S NAME, WHY?" He went back to upper case. "WHY!, WHY!"

"Listen to me, Patrick, you are my sweetheart. I'm going to marry you. Listen closely. When we went into that barracks, I felt something, I ..."

Patrick interrupted. "You felt a draft, a draft and you got mixed up with what happened here. That's all!"

"Don't interrupt again, sweetheart. I thought at first that it was a draft. It was a pulling, a... a... compulsion like. It said in my head, 'Stay, stay, stay'"

"Monica, you have a fever, we better get back to the group before someone starts to look for us."

"Patrick, I do not have a fever. I am perfectly sane and clear headed. You have known me for a long time, If you truly love me, you'll go help me with this."

It was a visible struggle. He actually paced back and forth. "Okay, Okay. Let me digest this."

He went into planning mode, "We'll come back tomorrow and really explore this place well. We'll look for a place for you to hide your crazy self. I don't guess that the watchmen here expect anybody to stay overnight. but I bet that some nuts other than you tried to."

To make a long story short, we casually asked our tour guide, like dumb American tourists, if any one wanted to or tried to, stay a night in Auschwitz.

"Not to my knowledge, Pan Callahan, Panni Kelly. All of the folks I've ever went with here were just plain terrified.

Europeans most of all. They know what happened not so far from them and want no part of doing anything except maybe a fast walk-through. On your side of the world people tend to be just a little more apt to consider things like staying here for a night, but that's all! Why? I must say that I would expect you Americans to try something dangerous like that." Marek, the guide said.

"Oh, no, no we may be Americans, but not that crazy. Why did you say 'dangerous'? Patrick asked.

"Dangerous to the head, the brain, the mind," Marek said. "You know what this place was, yes?"

"Oh, yes," we both replied. Forget we even asked." I hoped that we sounded sincere. Marek still regarded us as, if not crazy, then reckless and foolish Americans.

We went back the next day with a different guide and we eventually found a place for me to hide. It was in a space in back of an exhibit of material left behind by the doomed Jews.

Patrick made sure that I was dressed warmly, muttering to himself that he was as crazy as I was. We went back a third day, with a different shift at the gate office and just joined a group who were speaking Spanish. We tagged along with them, nodding and smiling. saying, "Sí, Sí", and getting some funny looks.

We drifted away from the group and headed toward the barracks and the hiding place. We waited for some folks to enter, folllowed them and Patrick stood in front of me as I cracked open the door, which for some reason was unlocked, slipped into the closet like space and sat down. The place smelled old and weird, like.

We knew what time the camp closed and night fell. I cracked open the door. No one was there the building was empty. I was too hyped up to feel scared, too much adrenaline. I went in to the barracks section and crawled into the top of the bunks and lie there. I made the sign of the cross and said two Hail Marys. That didn't help too much.

The compulsion had not left me. It simmered inside. A cold simmer.

Then I felt something like a not cold, not hot mist settle over me. A jumble of voices in what I recognized as Yiddish swirled around me. I wasn't afraid. I did not feel threatened.

I felt instead like my entire life's story was being absorbed by the mist, by the ten different entities* making up the mist. The Yiddish became English as each of the entities entered my mind. They found out that I was a virgin, which embarrased me but made one of them happy. The Rabbi, as I came to call that serene voice.

One voice said, "A virgin! Wow!"

"You putz! You're dead and all you can think of is sex?"

"So, maybe I'm more alive than dead?

"STOP IT, you idiots!" exclaimed the Rabbi. "A pure *neshuma* is absolutely necessary for this mission; especially a female one."

"Hey, what about a pure male *neshuma*?" I said, irritated. "You guys are so pure?"

"Sorry, sorry, I don't know why. Maybe it's because you are ...." the rabbi began.

"Never mind. No 'maybes' accepted," I replied, still irritated. "Move on."

The jumble of voices sorted themselves out. "Ah, an American, not a Polack. A young woman, yet! A CATHOLIC! OY! And what are we? Why are we? Gentlemen, calm down! Let your Rabbi conduct this, please."

Another jumble of voices. "A great surprise! What is she doing here? From the *goldeneh medina* yet. A Jew lover? A *mishoogenah*? Wait, let's calm down. We ourselves are here for some reason. Remember, I told you. She must be here for a reason. We will find out. *Baruch **HaShem**.*"

The points of lights arranged themselves in front of me. I was now lying on the floor.

"Listen," said the serene voice. "There is a reason she is here. We willl find it. Remember, *achim*, the first time we tried? Let me go *between*,"

His voice changed from English, as I heard it, into a language which I sensed was ancient, whch had a rhythm to it, a sensation of ancient days. Then his voice changed into English. "I have the answer, I am sure of it. The reason is: there is a connection, distant, but there, between our goal and Monyka."

"Wait a minute! Hiow did you come up with that so quick?" an entity asked.

"Noodnik, remember, I went into the *between* and studied"

"You and your 'between'," harrumphed another voice, "So nu, tell us already."

"We cannot accomplish our mission unless Monyka joins us; brings us her *neshumah*."

"How can that happen? Ten of us plus a non-Jewish female? Is this truly from **HaShem**, or from the Fallen One, may he suffer?"

"Remember how I refused to join with you at even though we knew what our mission was? When I was in the *between* this time, **HaShem** said to me - "let **Me** judge this matter. If I find some spark of *nefesh tov* there, all will be well. If not, eternal darkness. So, **I** am in accord with you. So join the minyan, Rabbi"

The points of light blinked out.

I, Monica/Monyka, remained alone in a barracks in Auschwitz, Poland, in March, 2019.

In March, 1943, ten men were part of forty men standing outside a barracks in a miserable, cold drizzle, answering the morning *appel* at 5:00 AM.

SS-Obersturmbannführer Artur Lebhenschel, commandant of Auschwitz (May 1940 to November 1943), was in a particularly foul mood, made worse by the foul weather. He crouched rather than sat in his box as he snarled out the numbers of the wretches lined up in front of him.

He stopped calling numbers and stared at the ragged bunch.

He suddenly leaped out of his box, causing the guards to point their weapons at the men from the barracks as if they were preparing to attack the officer.

"Nein, nein, alles gut" The Ober pointed out ten men in the first row. The guards pulled them out of line. They stood infront of the Ober.

"Schwein! Hast du meine schöne sprache deutsch geklaupt und schweinchen davon reden lassen!" he screamed, ripping his Lüger out of its holster and pointing it at the ten, *"Ir kokn tsu fil vi goyim, tsu fil! Nu, ikh redn dehn kahzir sprakh tsu shikn ir tsu genem! Ihr blut wird in den Boden eindrigen und für immer dort beiben, Schweine!"* He emptied his weapon into the ten. screaming, *"Genem! Genem!"*

The ten men dropped into ten piles of rags, the drizzle turning blood into pink rivulets which soaked into the ground.

After the initial shock, the guard prodded the rest of the men into the barracks and decided, like neat Nazis, to clean up the area.

"Nein! Lass sie liegn und verotten!" the Ober said. Then reloading his pistol, he stepped back into his box. he motioned a guard to get the men out of the barracks and he resumed his *appel* as if nothing at all had happened.

The guards were uneasy at this display of frenzy by the Ober, but did not dare to question him. A Jew must have done something really bad to him.

The ten lie there for three days. then they were thrown into the oven. The Ober thought that he had made his point. No pigs wanted. Their blood soaked into the ground.

That night the drizzle became a torrent. Lightning struck the electrified fence. The lights went out for an hour until the auxilliary generators kicked in.

The prisoners were made to fall out in the rain for appel and were counted again just to make sure that no one escaped during the black out. No one had.

The torrent subsided. A lightning bolt traveled from the fence into the mud where the ten had fallen. Blood and electricity and the torrent of hate and rage poured on the ten mingled in the mud.

Something happened. Ten faintly glowing, tiny points of light bubbled out of the mud, washed clean by the rain. The will-o-the wisps rose and driftedm toward the barracks, where they merged into the walls.

There were ten points of light which were now part of the barracks. Ten points of light which were ten men once. And, ten men, in the Jewish tradition, make up a *minyan,* ten men who can then pray in the synagogue.

Time murdered onward.

In 1945 Auschwitz was liberated. Nine out of the forty men in the Minyan's barracks were pulled from death out of the forty by the liberators. The survivors were helped to make their way to the *goldeneh medina.* There they went forth and multiplied.

The ten points of light diffused in the walls of the building remained there, waiting.

With the barracks empty, the building's groans and creaks were audible in the cold silence of the empty building. This stirred the ten points of light. They emerged from the walls and hovered over a top bunk.

"What happened? Where are we? What are we?" Came a babble of vibrations,

The rabbi spoke, "By the grace of HaShem we are here, in the place where we were murdered. I will tell you a story"

"What story? What are you talking about? How do you know? How? Why?" nine voices vibrated.

"The story of why we are here and what for. So *luzein shah* and listen." So the points of light listened.

The Rabbi spoke for a long time, in timelessness. He quoted Talmud and many Rabbi's teachings and commentaries. He said, "In summary, we are here to dispose of SS-Obersturmbannführer Arthur Liebenhenschel before he explodes again. His descendants will be totally insane unless we eliminate the bad seed. We are, in effect, a 'hit squad',"

You took so long to tell us that we are like an American gangster movie? A 'hit squad'?

A 'hit squad'? *Naarishkeit!* We are dead since two years! We can't even spit in his eye." said .... Why can't HaShem do it?"

"I do not know, but the **ALL POWERFUL** cannot!"

"Some all powerful. Why were we Jews subjected to the 'Final Solution' and the rest of the world all but cheered?" The all powerful wasn't so powerful, was he?

"I DO NOT KNOW! **HASHEM** WILL NOT ANSWER ME. I AM NOT THE FIRST WHO HAS QUESTIONED HIM. I WILL NOT BE THE LAST. WE WILL NOT BE THE LAST. HE WILL NOT LET ME SEE A RAINBOW.

"I know that we have a mission. He told me to be patient. We Jews know how to be patient. I do not know for what we wait." said the Rabbi.

"Nu, Rabbi, so here we are. What are we waiting for?"

"**Now**!" shouted the Rabbi. There was a second of great wind.

The minyan was back in 1943, the night before they were murdered.

"What we will do is make a trial run before we dispose of the Ober." said the Rabbi.

"A trial run of what?

"Of what we will do to the SS-Obersturmbannfürher. We will practice on a guard. We will concentrate our power and focus on a guard."

"Concentrate our power? What power?"

"That we will find out. Get ready,"

"Hey, wait a minute. Y'know, I am on the ground, dying and I wondered; why did that lunatic yell, 'tsu genem?' He must have picked up real high Yiddish. We'd say, 'Gey in dr'erd."

"What does that nonsense have to do with what we are just about to do?

"I don't know. I'm really nervous."

Ten dead men nervous!

It was night watch. Corporal Hans Gelber marched by, looking straight ahead. The ten points of light became a beam which focused on the back of the corporal's neck.

Corporal Gelber stopped, shuddered shook his head, muttered something in his Bavarian dialect and marched on.

The beam retreated into a shadow and resolved itself into ten points of light.

"Nothing! *Gurnisht*! The *momser* didn't even fart! What are we? Our trial run wasn't even a crawl!

The Rabbi said, "Now I know that we must become more powerful."

"More powerful?" "How, how in the name of HaShem?"

"NOW" shouted the Rabbi. There was a second of great wind.

The minyan was back in March, 2019.

I, Monica/Monyka was frozen there.

"Monyka, you are what we need. You have been sent to us by HaShem. You will help us to get rid of the Commandant of this place. You will make this piece of history less horrible." the Rabbi said to me.

"How can I help? A Christian, a girl? Ah! The neshuma thing!

"Yes, you are right! More will be explained. You are a vital part of our mission."

And the Rabbi told me every thing, every detail of what happened; the 'trial run' and everything. The minyan thought and hoped that they could do it, just the ten of them. But, no.

Then he told me something which made me shiver in disgust. My family was a twig on a branch of the Commandant's tree. Distant, but there.

"Monyka, we need your power, your pure *neshuma* to complete our mission. You will not be harmed. You will be fulfilled."

"No more compulsions? No more dark dreams"

"No, *shayna*. Only good dreams," said the Rabbi.

"Ready? Men? Monyka?"

"NOW!" shouted the Rabbi.

It was March, 1943.

Forty men stood in the cold drizzle while a Nazi officer sat in a box and called out numbers. The Nazi suddenly sprang from his box, had ten men dragged out in front of him, shouted at them and shot them down.

The next day, he sat in his box. he was calling out names.

Eleven points of light, nearly invisible in the drizzle, streamed into the box and focussed on the Nazi's neck. The beam reached down to his heart and rapidly squeezed it, gave it a final eleventh squeeze and withdrew, becoming a single point of light which hovered over the scene.

SS-Obersturmbannführer Arthur Liebenschel stood up, gargled a scream and fell out of the box flat on his face in the mud, almost on top of the ten bodies he shot three days ago. He lay still, mud on his Nazi uniform.

The guards, for once acting without a direct order, shoved every one of the prisoners back into the barracks and called for the Officer of the Day. The medics arrived and carted the body away. The ten bodies lay where they had fallen.

SS-Sturmbannführer Arthur Liebenschel died nobly for Die Führer in the line of duty, read the report.

The next day, SS-Sturmbannführer Richard Baer, (May 1944 to January 1945) took over and life dragged on.

It became March, 2019.

In the barracks, ten points of light coalesced each one into ten men. A minyan. Each dressed in the clothing they worn as free men. There arms were tattoo free. Then, each man became a shaft of pure light and launched straight up into the dawning sky. The last pure shaft of light bent toward Monica and kissed her on the forehead and ascended.

Monica woke. She had dreamed, a terrible but a dream which dissolved the compulsion. She heard a still voice in her head, "Baruch HaShem". Monyka became Monica.

She waited until a group of tourists came by, stopped and peered in horrified wonder at the exhibit and started to move on. She cracked open the door and quietly slipped into the tail end of the group. She casually made it to the front gate. Faithful Patrick was there.

They left Poland with a souvenir or two.

They returned to Waltham, Mass., got married, and had two boys and two girls. The children were given the names of those victims of the Holocaust, which they studied, as good Christians.

Patrick worked for IBM and they lived well. Monica took classes in library science, became Chief Librarian of the Massachussetts Public Library. Her research indicated that her family was indeed a very distant relative of the SS Nazi son of a bitch who had a 'heart attack'.

Records indicate - the Nazis kept meticulous records - that the next commandant of Auschwitz, SS-Sturmbannführer Richard Baer took over until the camp was liberated. He fled and was later captured by the Israelis in 1993 and hanged in Israel.

Korporal Hans Gelber said that enough was enough and committed suicide in 1946.

Monica, 2029.

Over the next ten years, I remembered more and more of what happened. I found the village and area the minyan came from. If you are interested, I can supply a biography of each one of the men who became ascending shafts of light. Their names are recorded in Yad VaShem in Jerusalem.

A blip in history? A *bubbameiseh*? I picked up that word in my research.

Monica Callahan

NOTES

Monica and Patrick names alone were changed.

The ten points of light, the 'minyan' were Jewish men from the same town and suroundings. Ordinary. Middle aged. Their families were lost in other concentration camps. The only voice that spoke with authority was that of Rabbi Heinz Alt. The others remained nine unidentified voices, nine minyanim. They were:

2. Norbert Darliki. 3. Rudolf Brumlik. 4. Bronislaw Chamez. 5. Benjamin Fondanski. 6. Miroslav Shalom. 7. Kurt Gerron. 8. Petr Gint. 9. Pavel Haas.

Neshumah is used here to mean the essence of a soul.

"Schwein!..........reden lassen." **German:** "You have stolen my beautiful German language and turned it into pig talk." "Ir koken ... genemen." You look too much like Christians. See I can speak your pig talk and you can go to hell." **Yiddish.** "Ihr blut .... Schweine!" Your blood will stay in the earth forever, Pigs!" **German**.

The Oberst used the third person singular because he regarded the ten as one unit.

"Baruch HaShem": **Hebrew,** Bless The Name. Instead of saying 'God'.

nefesh tov: A spark of good.

Between: A timeless dimension accessible only to those who have inherited a genetic key, where minds are free to seek answers and consult other seekers as well as the Highest One.

THE LUNCH BOX

I name myself Mervin Marde for this narrative. I am a Private Investigator, operating solo as MervEye Investigations.

I am thirty five, 5'9", good head of black hair going grey, no facial hair, trim musculature, six-pack abs still defined. No other six packs; I don't drink, except for an occasional Shirley Temple. Brown eyes, often refered to as squinty by my detractors and focused by my lady friends. Nice blue suit, shirt, tie. I think that blue is my favourite colour.

I never married, both to spare my wife and children from the vicissitudes of a PI's life: staying awake during stake outs, avoiding domestic squabbles, which rarely were settled without the intermediary getting affected in some way. For "affected", read "getting hurt".

Sometimes, in the right light, my features have a Far Eastern look about them. I've wondered about that, but not much. I was adopted by a great mostly Caucasian family and, as mentioned, for the purposes of this ongoing saga, named myself Mervin Marde in order to protect my adopted family.

Even as a trained investigator, I never felt the need to piece together the jigsaw puzzle of my own life. My foster parents were all that I wanted.

I also volunteer as a Meals on Wheels driver for the Blake County Social Services Department once a week. I also visit MoW - men folks - once a week or sometimes more, who have no other contacts. MoW knows this; I do not accept anything from them, do any personal errands (Social Servics does that). We just chat and I sometimes listen to tales of long ago and far away I make sure that I am not mentioned in any such things as last wills and testaments. I do this because of professional ethics. I want nothing from those who have next to nothing. Or nothing.

The following unfolding of events takes place on my regular Wednesday run when a new recipient was added to my list of people who receive MoWs. I shall attempt to make this a cohesive story.

Assam Draggin is my last stop. He answers the door after I announce. "Meal on Wheels" loudly.

He wears a richly embroided caftan and a fez. He's a stooped 6'5". That I can tell because if he straighted up, the fez would hit the door frame. I noticed, after the mild shock at his appearance - I've seen many door openers in many costumes or lack of same in both my vocation and avocation.

He had a well tended gray handlebar of a moustache attached under a well shaped, unbroken nose, really blue eyes and a lined, light complexioned face. I couldn't tell what the rest of him looked like because of the caftan. Age difficult to ascertain. Mid seventies?

As we both stood there, I noticed that the caftan and fez were of a certain worn and faded elegance - a prince in exile, perhaps. Still able to command attention. He actually straightend up to regard me, the fez nearly knocked off his head by the door lintel.

"Ah. Meals on Wheels", I stammered.

"Thank you, young man. Mi casa es su casa. Enter, please. and welcome." He said in a well modulated baritone.

Pleasant voice; accent difficult to place. English may not have been his first language. His "th" and "z" were pronounced correctly; his 'w' not a 'v'.

"I'd like to, Mr. Draggin, but I have to move on, other -ah- customers, y'know. I'll take a rain check."

Even though he was the last on my list, I didn't want to

accept his invitation until I had done a background check. I noticed through the open door that the room seemed cluttered with what looked like exotic bricabrac.

I thought that I saw a something luminous around the mantel piece, a box or a square object on the mantel piece. But whatever it was disappeared when I actually focused my gaze on it. Maybe whatever Assam was smoking affected me because I noticed a hookah in the middle of the floor with a spiral of smoke coming from it.

"I understand, indeed," he replied. 'Rain check' interesting expression, that. Well, thanks for the lunch box, even though it's on a tray and wrapped in cling film. I find 'lunch box' an interesting expression as well."

Cling film? That's a British English expression.

"Hey, I'll be glad to talk about both phrases, real soon," I stepped back and he closed the door softly.

Well, I thought. He sounds like a cool subject for research.

So, when I got back to the MoW building and handed in my visit sheet, I sloped along to my inherited condo in North Rawley and started to plunge into Assam's life. I used all the methods at my disposal, most of which were quite legal, and came up with the following:

Assam (NMI) Draggin was born on 1 April in either 1910 or 1920. The '1' or '2' in the date seemed to have been blurred on the translated copy of his birth certificate. Curious.... He did look well preserved no matter the blurred number.

He was born in Shakranistan of Tachat and Nalga Draggin, both of whom were small shop owners specializing in antiquities. They wound up in West Carolina as political refugees because they were of the wrong political party, which was not so anti-government as the fact that they sold ancient artifacts made in China yesterday. The authorities were annoyed because those "antiquities" were giving Shakranistan an even worse reputation as a tourist trap than they already had.

The Draggins were allowed to leave with 100 Kapoks in cash and the clothes on their backs. The government confiscated the "antiquities" and later sold them to tourists together with certificates of authenticity also printed in China.

They left with the infant Assam. and the box, of which they were the guardians. They told the Shakrani authorities that the box contained the ashes of their ancestors, which guaranteed a safe passage, since the Shakranis were ancestor worshippers, among other things. The Draggins actually didn't know what was in the box.

The three were granted legal status and were lent some start-up money for entrepreneurs. They looked around downtown Rawley, and with the help of the start-up dollars, were able to lease a storefront and started to build a stock of "Knitted by Nalga" Shakrani sleeveless jackets. They sold well, but not well enough.

The Draggins developed a formidable, unrelenting case of nostalgia and decided to go back to Shakranistan. The American diet was too rich for them, even if they tried to arrange for Shakrani foods. Since the ingredients were grown in the USA, the dishes were but pale copies of "real" food.

They decided that Assam would do better to stay in America, so they asked a neighboring shop keeper couple, who were childless, if they would adopt Assam, since they could not expect Assam to thrive in a country of which he knew nothing. The shopkeepers really were fond of the toddler and applied to adopt Assam. Thety were vetted and found suitable. Assam kept his Shakrani name to honour his parents. A first for the Draggins.

They opened another antiquities shop in Cortch, the

capital, featuring artifacts from ancient Shakranistan which were actually made in the country.

Assam inherited the one thing that Tachat had managed to smuggle out of the country: the box, which did not contain ashes. It was the box on the mantel. That lunch box which continued to fascinate me. I must find out why!

Assam grew up rather well adjusted to life in West Carolina and following in his parent's footsteps. He became an antiquities dealer of authentic ancient artifacts with certificates made yesterday in China. He rented a storefront in Cameroff Village to regale natives and tourists with the provenance of each ancient artifact and oddity. His sign in vivid colours in English and Esperanto read "Curiosities of the World. Enter and find out what you are curious about".

He did roam the world many times to acquire non-Chinese made items, leaving his business in the hands of a trusted non-Shakrani who came with very good references from other employers. However, Mr. Hu Goniv turned out to have forged his references. When Hu felt that he had made enough money from the business, he simply cashed out the enterprise, gave away the antiquities at rock bottom prices, plus a small shipping and handling fee, and fled.

Hu covered his tracks exceedingly well. He decided that the authorities would not really follow up on a mere victimless robbery and spare themselves the endless paperwork and maybe follow ups. Hu scarpered off to a remote somewhere and presumably lived out his life if not in the lap of luxury, in its bosom. So the case just faded away.

Upon his return to West Carolina and Rawley, Assam found that he was ruined. The only thing remaining was the cigar box, which Assam called the lunch box, as it is to be called henceforward in this narrative. He had hidden it in the floor of his business near a rack of plastic Eiffel towers which remained covered in ever increasing layers of dust, since nobody had ever evinced interest in the display, not even Francophiles.

The ancient artifacts were manufactured of soapstone in China, carefully aged to resemble artifacts from the Hoder/ Chingau dynasties. They were designed to crumble into soap powder in two years so that Assam could claim deniability and blame the manufacturers. He told his customers that he could only apologize for Hu Goniv's thievery. He washed his hands of the whole business. He replaced the artifacts sold during Hu's time with new ancient artifacts comissioned from China. These were more exotic items designed to crumble in three years.

Assam applied for and obtained Welfare in due course. He was also placed on the Meals on Wheels program, where he was assigned to me.

I continued to visit Assam once a week and formed a friendship with him. I did feel at times that he was more than a friend. I told the MoW folks that I would visit Mr. Draggin when I had a chance because he really needed a listener in the flesh, not Instagram, Twitter, Facebook, You Tube or any other virtual reality contacts. Besides, after the first month of the above social media outlets, he hurled his PC at the screen. It then just sat there and sulked.

During the off-MoW visits, I even shared his bubble pipe with him. It turned out that he smoked a mixture of tumbleweed, oregano and a half button of grown-in China peyote. Not a bad combination. It gave one the sensation of rolling around in a desert in the Old West, being in a salad and smoking a Peace Pipe. The resulting high lasted long enough to recite a few dirty limericks. Assasm intones his in Shakrani, which he told me he memorized without quite knowing what the verses meant. He assumed that they were rather raunchy. and I recited The Signifyin' Monkey, a folk legend. Since none of understood the other, we had a high old time.

I was prompted to investigate more thoroughly the backgrounds of his parents, Tachat and Nalga. Using my proven PI methods. I discovered that Tachat actually had a cousin in a tiny town in the hills of West Carolina called Inchest. His name was Ahmo Sinandi, which he did not Americanize because of his business, manufacturing and selling fertility idols, not gods, which might offend the Inchesters, who were fervid Fundamentalists and rather liked Ahmos. Idols were OK, since everyone knew that Father Abraham busted up his dad's idols. So the citizens of Inchest bought the idols and then had a community bust-up during Christmas during which they shattered the idols and used the shards to fill potholes. And bought more idols.

Ahmo married Morwena Blanca, a local. They had a child, Fimbulwinter. He had as normal a childhood as a kid could have who grew up in an idol shop. He was home schooled, since there were no schools in Inchest; their progeny being instructed either at home, or in the halls of learning in nearby Prognosis.

Fimbulwinter left home as soon as he reached majority at sixteen and dropped off the radar. Inchest was just too small for his ambitions. He wanted to do more than sell fertility idols.

But I would trace him doggedly, using every means at my disposal. Now THAT took a bunch of time, tracing bits of documents and records and even sources that smacked of sorcery. I found that Fimbulwinter married Sittinshiva, an Ivrit Indian girl from Kerala. Now they had a boy child that they had to give up for adoption because Fimbulwinter and Sittinshiva just couldn't make it on Fimbulwsinter's wages as an apprentice artificer and Sittinshiva's as a bustle framer.

They saved their money and traveled into obscurity in Pergola, a town in central Italy, where artificers and bustle framers went to retire.

The boy bounced from household to household, all black haired, browneyed little boy, not badly treated, finally named Argon by his last "parents". I traced Argon and found something which blew my mind.

I went into deep shock for a month or two because of what I found I couldn't believe it.

I operated purely automatically, attending to my business, chatting with my people of MoW.

Smoking with Assam, who realized that something was not right but wisely did not push me. My training as a PI helped me assimilate the fact the I was Shakrani by DNA, or whatever spiral I was connected to. Why the shock?

Because, all tests verified, I was Argon. I WAS ARGON! I WAS ARGON!!

Me, Mervin Marde iof MerveEye Private Investigator. I was actually related to Assam! I checked and rechecked the advanced technology which lead to my relation to Assam. Same results. No mistakes. None!

That hubble-bubble really helped dissolve my shock. I could focus now on the mysterious box on the mantel. During my visits, official and off the clock with Assam, I talked my way closer and closer to the topic of that luminous - to me - box on the mantel piece. He would slide around the box topic, circling around the lunch box conversationally.

Assam had never seen the luminousity or felt the warmth when I managed to touch it that once. He just regarded it as an heirloom to be cherished.

"Look, Assam, we and science both have confirmed that I am related to you - a cousin, or what ever. if you aren't that curious about the lunchbox, please, I beg of you, let me hold it. Let me feel the warmth."

"Well, since you now are family - okay. You've been like a brother to me anyway. I gotta tell you that all I did was keep that lunchbox, I never really examined it. Something kept me from doing it. I don't know what. I tried to open it, but I got a shock! So I actually spoke to the box and told it that I would leave it alone! So it just sat on my mantel and sulked. How do you like that? Two sulkers in my house!"

I reverently took the "lunchbox" off the mantel. No shock! I examined it more closely with a magnifying glass that I wore around my neck on a stainless steel chain. It was made of a substance with which I was unfamiliar. It was unclassifiable. It actually wasn't luminous; the enamel reflected ambient light. The warmth remained a mystery. My mini-Geiger counter, made in Paraguay, was silent. The box was constructed in pieces joined together like an Incan wall. It was inscribed in a number of languages, one of which I recognized: Spanish! It read "Not made in China. Proudly constructed in Cortch, the capital of Shakranistan". What the other languages said might have been the same thing.

One tiny illustration, enlarged by the magnifying glass showed the lunchbox disassembled. By the bollocks of Baal! It was actually a non-Chinese puzzle box! Still, one must manipulate various pieces to solve the puzzle and open the box.

I turned and turned the box, I examined it minutely. I discerned minute numbers on each piece. The opening formula! Was one to press the pieces in sequence? 1,2,3 etc? Could it be that simple? Let's try it!

I pushed each numbered piece in sequence and VOILA! It worked the first time! Some mystery!! Okay, but why me. Was I Chosen to open the thing?

One of the pieces had an inlay. It was a coin! A gold coin the diameter of an American double eagle. There was a spot on the grooved rim which looked like lead. Another piece of the puzzle had strange writing on it which blurred before my eyes and metamorphosed into English, or perhaps it was in English all along? The writing stated that the coin, called a Zxyqcz, was the result of a formula which changed lead into gold - the mythical Philosopher's Stone. The lead spot was to show that the coin actually was once all lead. There was only one other Zxyqcz, indicated the words on another piece of the puzzle. That coin was in the Schmitsonian in DC and was half lead!

The formula was scattered on the rest of the pieces of the puzzle lunch box. I did not want to find it. I felt that it was better the formula stayed fragmented. It was not for me, ever.

The reason I was able to open and decipher the writing on the lunchbox was because I was the last drop of the Draggins, no matter how my genes were mixed and spliced. Go figure! Assam was prohibited from opening the box, serving only as guardian until the Chosen One appeared. He was just too much of a con man, even for the Shakranis, to be chosen as the Chosen One. It was fitting that he be the Guardian, nothing more. He was Shakrani, after all.

Assam disclosed something else and said that he was sorry for not telling me before:

it appeared that a Chosen One declared that he was the One had come from Korea. When he approached the vicinity of the box on the mantel, he was immediately dissolved into molecules and frozen in the Ozone Layer, where his molecule of Frozen Chosen imposter drifted to Earth intermitently as fertilizer.

Asam and I palavered long and deply about the disposition of the Zxyqcz. We finally came to the conclusion that the Schmitsonian could keep it as a permanent loan, not to display, but to keep it in the reassembled lunchbox. I did not inform them of the Philosopher's Stone formula which was too well hidden to be uncovered by any present technology. The Schmitsonian pledged to advance Assam and me, Argon, a princely sum annually as we prepared to ride off into the sunset, to enjoy a retirement full of pulchritude and Mimosas.

So. Assam got off Welfare and MoWs, I deeded over my PI business to Monocular Polis, a well qualified ex-policeman and optometrist. We took the first briefcase full of real American and Euro cash monies and bought a sea going yacht.

We sailed from an undisclosed location in order to avoid any obstacle to our departure toward Cramalot, an island paradise in a neighboring dimension. So we weighed anchor and sailed away with fair winds and following seas.

Our remittance from the Schmitsonian was forwarded to a Swiss bank, which handled it from Lake Geneva.

I am writing this from Cramalot, where many faiths are crammed together only in theology. We have plenty of physical space. We exist in utmost, perfect harmony.

Once in a while, a recovering athiest throws a party. We can attend, or retreat to our personal solitude if we don't wish to party.

We never regreted not using the Philosopher's Stone formula.

PAX VOBISCUM!!

NASCAR IT WASN'T

There are at least 100 types of manned (or womend) motorized wheelchairs, scooters and walkers in existence in America, not counting the ones used elsewhere in the world, with new configurations on the horizon.

Most of the above are in use in RiverRun Senior Apartments.

We do not now pilot one of these configurations; rather, we are in constant danger of being T-boned, sideswiped, grazed, blindsided or otherwise physically challenged by their physically challenged drivers. Unintentionally, for the most part, except for the ancients who are reliving their youth and/or second childhood as daredevil speedsters. These actually aim for us. We and other residents are still able to dodge them while, unaware, we are backing into other Fountain of Youth seekers. We have learned to zig-zag like springboks or gazelles being chased by cheetahs.

To channel the agressive tendencies of these ancient navigators, we decided to organize corridor races with motorized wheelchairs in competiton against each other, with other chargers to come next. Prizes would be awarded, to be determined by the winner's personal physicians.

The corridors in RiverRun are long enough and wide for two operators. It didn't take much persuasion to recruit squads of eager drivers, since they already had their competitive buddies. The more conservative amongst the RiverRunners preferred to be observers.

The management at first proved difficult to agree, citing a library of legalities against such a proposal. We fianally brought them around after detailing the precautions taken: just a trial run at first, no press, padding along the walls, helmets, a top speed of two miles an hour, EMT teams stationed at strategic points along the corridor course. The staff would cheer them on. Such an event would be a fantastic PR coup for RiverRun.

A day was selected for the motorized wheelchairs. Two drivers, so bundled up that their gender was unknown, mounted, lined up side by side to await the starting flag.

Flag up, flag waving, flag down. The race drivers hurtled like turtles down the coridor, each putting pedal to metal, screaming either encouragement or ancient obscenities at each other.

The commentator went ballistic describing the racers as each foot of the course was consumed under the wheels of the drivers. It was a photo finish!

Unfortunately, the camera at the finish line malfunctioned and the winner was officially never determined.

Press coverage was favorable:

"Pops Pop a Wheelie" "Gearshft Granny Grabs the Gold"

The unofficial non-photo finish winner was the Widder Gummer, who actually grabbed the gold plated zinc medal from Gramps Dribbler. She claimed that she had won by a footrest and demanded that those attachments be measured on each motor. Results were indeterminate, since an argument ensued whether or not wear and tear should be considered. The controversey petered out when the Widder and Grumps dozed off. The Widder wore the medal around her neck for a long, long time.

But we digress.The races became wildly popular, The Russians tried to introduce "troika" racing, The Australians trained kangaroos to drive customized wheelchairs. Both efforts had limited success. But that's another story. People tried to evade and fake the age limit; no one under seventy five admitted. No doping tests were held. All contestants were chock full of prescription drugs normally.

Franchises were sold. RiverRun exploded wih new housing. The handicapped-motorized-auxilliary ambulatory-devices industry raced to the top of their graphs.

The fad died down to weekly short sprints on daytime TV when new events captured the public's fickle fancy.

Sky diving with umbrellas, breathing asbestos, chewing tea bags - especially in the UK - lingered for a time and faded into the mists of the past, remaining as footnotes in thousand page reference books.

But the ghosts of Widder Gummer and Gramps Dribbler haunt the original RiverRun building, zooming up and down the corridors, cackling at each other.

You must stand witness to these occurrences some 0-dark-thirty hours in the AM.

THE HALLOWEEN CAPER

This story is about how Detective Lieutenant (DL) Anastasia Amanda Romanova, PhD, handled the Halloween Caper.

On 1 November 2019, the following incident occurred on Halloween Eve, 31 October, 2019 at Riverrun Senior Repository, Raleigh, NC.

Mr. Pinchas O'Nion Moriarty, 93, was found deceased, seated in his "Jazzy" motorized wheelchair which had hit the wall at the end of the corridor by apartment 221B, which was occupied by Messrs Hemlock Sholmes PhD, retired apiarist and Ivan Batson, MD.

Mr. Moriarty's passing took place at midnight, Halloween Eve, 31 October, 2019.

Messrs Sholmes and Batson stated that they heard a "thump" at midnight, opened their door and discovered the deceased up against the wall. Dr. Batson declared him dead upon testing for a pulse. Mr. Moriarty had been scheduled at 221B for his annual checkup and a discussion of his hypochondria. The late night appointment was not that unusual, since Mr. Moriarty was an owl spotter. Messsrs S. and B. were night folk as well, Hemlock working on a filter so that he could filter out the urban glare and count Nebulae. Dr. Batson was cataloging wild Turpentines, who roamed at night. They enjoyed Moriarty's tales of his exotic and erotic adventures in various parts of the world, like the Province of The Bronnix in Transistria, which balanced the litany of his aches and pains.

DL Romanova responded to the 911 call made by the Manager, Mason Suthren. On arriving at the scene and upon preliminary examination, DL Romanova agreed with Dr. Batson as to the deceased's corporeal status.

DL Romanova did not notice any external trauma until the EMT removed the deceased from his chair and laid him on a stretcher. She then noticed that Mr. Moriarty's facial features expressed extreme terror.

DL Romanova considered the time and place of the fatal event and considered that perhaps Mr. Moriarty actually was scared to death or scared himself to death. Preliminary assessment, heart failure. Yes, but what scared him?

Both Hemlock and Ivan, upon viewing Mr. Moriarty, observed that the deceased looked "scared to death".

Being scared to death? A Halloween practical joke gone wrong?

Mechanical failure?

Moriarty's motorised wheelchair was the latest manufactured by Jazzy: cold fusion powered, 250 lbs., leather cushioned, fully maneurverable, with headlights and other accessories. Not inexpensive by a long shot. The driver's manual is quite thick.

DL Romanova requiested that she be shown the deceased's apartment forthwith. More about Mr. Suthern later.

His will was in a drawer, clearly marked "Last Will and Testament of Pinchas O'Nion Moriarty. It specified that his photographs of the world's waterfalls be donated to the Smithsonian. Any cash assets was to be given to a Miss Irene Adler, who was, to quote Mr. Moriarty: "A fabulous lay." "The rest of my assets; furniture, books and tchotskes to whatever family shows up at my cremation."

The Jazzy? It was customised to fit him, but many of his peers, male and female, were of the same physical characteristics, and the Jazzy was not engineered to function by fingerprint or voice ID. Anyone could pilot the machine.

That seemed inconsistent with custom fitting; that practically anyone could use the Jazzy. Mr. Mason Suthren, General Manager of Riverrun was designated to see to its disposition. Forensics would determine if the insertion of Mr. Southren's name in the will seemed to be added later.

Jealously as a motive? Mr. PM did have a reputation as a Don Juan amongst the female residents. He was often heard to say that there may be snow on his roof, but there was a cozy fire downstairs. His was, he bragged, a fine structure. Some ladies did inducate an architectural interest in him.

Twin sisters Jane and Emma Austen both inclined toward him, but they both expressed no interest in Mr. Moriarty's means of propulsion; it had simply too many bells and whistles for them. Ms. Belle Poitrine proffessed an initial interest in the ability of Mr. Moriarty to engage in various actions, but then backed off (literally) in her motor when Mr. M's ability to navigate in his out-of- his-Jazzy-mode proved less than advertised.

In the course of her investigation, Anastasia had to interview residents who lived on different floors. The elevators were more centrally located than the staircases and provided more interaction with the residents who plied Anastasia with hints of conspiracy as they piled into the elevators with walkers, four pronged canes and motorized wheelchairs.

Of course, the stairs could not be navigated by drivers of the various mechanisms employed to facilitate mobility. They were meant for staff, visitors and various extra-elevator events, snogging, perhaps.

Walking through the corridors was a challenge, since the coridors were 60" wide. The walkers were 18" - 20" wide, not counting the outstanding elbows. Getting past the sometimes glacially slow paced of the drivers was almost impossible; an exercersize in ballet. The mechanisms and pilots invariably inched down the center of the coridor, leaving 20" inches on either side to squeeze past. Elbows narrowed the space. The drivers also zigzagged as they snailed along. One way was to say in a commanding, outside voice, "coming through", and hope that the driver heard one. Pushing them aside was unacceptable, startling and rude. Such actions may cause a heart attack. Getting as close as possible and screaming "I've got to pee" helps on occasion. The driver might answer, "so do I" and actually increase speed a fraction of an inch, which don't help much if the screamer actually has to pee.

Following the person and attempting to zig when they zagged wasn't that successful, since the followed seem to have a dimensional sense of space and zigged at the same time the follower zigged, which, when seen overhead, made for a duo of zig zaggers down the corridors, which semed miles long when one actually had to pee. Or keep an appointment with a resident, who might be asleep if the interviewer was more than five minutes late. When there were two walkers sailing along at turtle warp speed, chatting to one another, with Anastasia, for example, behind, a bookie would not take odds on a successful pass.

The words "driver" and "pilot" are used interchangeably here for vehicle operators, since the owners of such exhibited many times the characteristics of race course racers and stunt pilots.

There was one resident, on a frame, who seemed to target Anastasia and scoot in front of her with suspicious regularity and matched zig for zag. Anastasia found herself unable to avoid her and took to asking her official guide, the manager Mr. Mason Suthren, to be on the lookout for The Forerunner, as she was known. It only worked some of the time; since recessed doorways were good spots for ambushing. The

Forerunner had lookouts as well to spot Anastasia's probable trajectory.

Anastasia could imagine races featuring the various mechanical ambulatory aides. A duo of one type of mechanism actually speeding down the corridor, perhaps sideswiping one another. A race between cane wielders would prove interesting. The caners would lengthen their stride and achieve a foot every 60 seconds. Quite a spectacle, Anastasia imagined.

Back to the Halloween Caper, if you please. The chastened Manager very willingly supplied biographies of the residents. Chastened? This willingness ensued because Mr. Suthren was told in no uncertain terms to "Keep his grubby hands off me or I'd break your fingers one by one and jam them down your throat or up elsewhere." Mr. Suthren stammered his apologies and said that it was merely an accident that he had managed to place his hands in inappropriate places. Anastasia would take no further action because she actually needed this slick, slim, full off himself, handsome, blond, dark of eye Manager for a while.

Manager Suthren was actually smart enough to keep his hands off female residents because he didn't want to lose his job. He did not want to lose his job, which had perks and bennies which he enjoyed. He had at least two girlfriends outside of Riverrun

So far, there was no actual person of interest (suspect) and it might be that Mr. Moriarty really did die of fright.

Further investigation, carried out by the DL, revealed that there were portraits along the walls of the corridors, said portraits appeared to move when the corridor lights flickered because of a surge of electricity. That Halloween night, the power appeared to flickered irregularly at the time Mr. Moriarty was going to visit the retired apiarist and friend for a checkup and a chew and chat.

Riverrun had to close down that corridor of the building because every Halloween there was a reenactment of Mr. Moriarty's demise by playful residents and the spirit of Mr. Moriarty. The residents of that floor were removed to another space and were given slow-descent toilet seats as compensation for their forced move.

The layout of apartment 221B was such that it was possible to make another opening into another corridor and seal up the original entrance. So the inhabitants did not have to move. The new corridor was named Baker Street; others of that section were Fisher Street, Pilot Street, Plantagenet Street and so forth. The new address of Messrs Sholmes and Batson then was 221B Baker St.

Let's just look at motives.

Were the twins Jane and Emma actually responsible for Pinchas's death, possibly Bella Poitrine? Did the flickering light play its part? Was there a third party to power Mr. Moriarty to his demise?

Belle Poitrine admitted that she had a crush on Pinchas, "I know that he was a ladies' man and that every time there was a new female resident, he was right there with his shit-eating grin and an invitation to guide them around the premises if they were willing to sit in his "side-car": his lap. Some ladies actually took him up on his offer. Few actually completed the tour; he was a "handy man of an old goat", they said, but he tired easily.

Everyone's alibi proved valid. Since nothing could be proven one way or the other, the case was thusly closed, stating that the decedent had apparently scared himself to death and his Jazzy drove itself down the corridor until smacking against the corridor wall.

The official verdict was "Death by Misadventure". Anastasia really couldn't reconcile that with what she felt instinctively, but the final verdict was above her pay grade, politics (Riverrun's reputation as a senior repository and connections) having a big part in the decision to close the case.

Anastasia felt compelled to revisit the scene of the event. She returned a few moths after the Halloween Caper. She looked at herself in Riverrun's ladies bathroom after successfully avoiding the Forerunner. She wondered if that compulsion showed. She had to admit to herself that she was rather outstanding.

She had café-au-lait skin, was blue eyed, black haired, 5'10" and quite shapely, according to her male squad mates. And not so visibly, Jewish. The latter gave her an instant in with many of the resident yentas who thought that she was an Ethiopian Jew.

When she was actively investigating the case, she thought that she looked like a cinammon stick in a cup of powdered sugar, old grey/white heads and short, bald pates stwirling around her like boiled peanuts in the cup. She wondered what what a caked baked from that mixture would look like. And taste.

As mentioned, she felt a compulsion to reasses the verdict of Death by Misadventure. The last two rooms of the corridor, formerly occupied by Mr. Sholmes and Dr. Batson, was now converted to storage space.

She just stood there, attempting to feel something. Nothing. She concentrated, calling forth the essence of Pinchas, not believing that anything would come of it.

Something touched her shoulder. She jumped a foot, spun around and almost shot Mr Suthren.

"For God's sake, don't shoot, don't shoot. You know me, Mason Manager, er Suthren," he stuttered. "All I wanted to know is, what are you doing here?"

"Sorry, Suthren. You remember me, don't you, man of

many hands? I'm revisiting the Pinchas O'Nion Moriarty case. It isn't closed to me"

"That was a while ago," he replied. "We have moved forward, DL, and are now rated five stars among senior repositories. Ah, so just what brings you here, DL?"

"I told you, I'm reviewing the Pinchas O'Nion case. Suthren, what are *you* doing here? The case is closed, ya know. And come to think of it, where is Mr. M's motorised mechanism.? The Jazzy? I didn't hear anything about it until you received it for storage. Where is it?"

"Ah, well, it ah." he muttered.

"Show me, Suthren, NOW! You always admired that Jazzy. Now, MOVE!"

"Lissen, lisssen, Ms. DL Ma'm. It's in the shop for repairs." Suthren beseeched whiningly.

"Yeah, sure." You saw me and figured my visit had something to do with Mr. Moriarty, didn't you? Anastasia whipped out her Glock and jammed it between Mason Suthren's eyes. Lord, she thought, I drew a gun on this crud! She hastily reholstered it and patted Suthren on the forehead. "Tell me true, Mason bubbelah, tell me true!"

The terrified Mason backed against the wall, his hair in disarry. "Don't shoot, don't shoot! I keep it in my house. I love it! I treasure it I take care of it. I'm gonna marry it!" he whimpered. "That dried out old mummy Moriarty didn't need it and he teased me all the time just because I kept lookin' at the thing. I figured that the old bugger had a heart issue because he'd go up to 221B alla time."

Anastasia thought that maybe marriage to a machine was what would just suit Suthren, but a life term in a psychiatric ward would preclude that.

"So, Suthren, you used the stairs, snuck up on Mr. Moriarty, hollered BOO in his ear, jammed his gear in first and sent him down the corridor. And if that wasn't enough, you used your flashlight and flickered it on and off on the portraits and scared him more in case the BOO wasn't enough!"

"Okay, Suthren, hands behind your back and get ready for the perp walk through Riverrun!"

"I want a lawyer. I wasn't there. I didn't do anything. Nobody saw me! You forced a fake confession from me by waving a cannon in my face!"

"Yeah, and you gunna marry a wheelchair with a motor."

""That's no ordinary machine, it's my fiancé." Suthren screamed as they walked through the lobby. Many of the residents watched the parade in fascination. Some waved at their departing Manager. Others saw nothing out of the ordinary.

Anastasia recieved a commendation and a promotion. Ex-Manager Suthren lived out his life worshipping a photo of his Jazzy. the Jazzy went to the Smithsonian. His girlfriends visit him from time to time, individually and separately.

The End

BREAK THE FAST

Break the Fast at RiverRun is a veritable geriatric ballet from 7:30 AM to 9:00 AM.

It is performed by a troupe of silent electric wheelchairs, noisier pushers and walkers, and their septo/octo/nonagenerian pilots who execute intricate arabesques designed to target everyone in the vicinity as well as fellow pilots. It staged in the area outside the dining hall.

Movements follow the entire range of classic ballet: leaping, spinning, en pointe and sidestepping on the part of those who are ambulatory with perhaps a cane as balancing rod. The mechanized actors are in the wings, primed to enter.

When those maneuvers are complete, when the initial dance macabre prior to entering the dining hall is complete, with a minimum of contusions, the queueing up begins.

One does this by queueing up behind the electric wheelchairs, walkers and pushers.Thus commences a glacially slow movement toward the counters of food. The resident spoons into a bowl one of various dry cereals, chooses skim or whole milk, all with precision and near Kelvin motion. Then the person chooses and attacks with the ferocity of an angry snail the chef's choice of the day, be it eggs and bacon, sausages, SoS or various components of a nutritious breakfast, followed by the selection of a plate, a choice of grits or oatmeal. The portions are ladled into the plates and placed on the seat of a rollator with the utmost precision and the speed of an alpha sloth.

All pilots then return to their seats, arranging their dining choice upon the tables. There is a surge toward the coffee urns and the pastry counter, with cups being filled and pastries chosen at negative light speed. There is a modicum of jostlings at these stations, the sinuous moves belying the arthritis of many diners.

When that task is accomplished, the pilots place their ambulatory aid where it most effciently impedes traffic flow. They proceed to break the fast with the alacrity of a sleepwalking turtle. Those who have completed their ingestion of the morning meal and are self-ambulatory, perhaps aided by a cane, then negotiate the maze of parked mechanisms by means of slipping and subtly shifting past those impediments in moves worthy of a Pavlova or a Nureyev. A Pavlova or a Nuryyrv as seen through a glass darkly.

Then the room gradually empties, the geriatric troupe retiring to recharge their batteries and grease up their pushers and walkers, preparing for another joust.

This refers to the breakfast hour only. The evening meal has its "rush hour" in a different fashion, with the clans gathered outside the dining hall, with some jostling for position, the hum of conversation swelling to a roar as the file of mechanisms and their occupants are ushered into the dining hall and seated at table and served. Once they are seated, the servers see to the placement of the residents mechanical aides into spaces which will not impede free passage to and from the kitchen.

Serving the meal mirrors sometimes the characteristics of the diners: slow. Then the waitstaff disappears! One must swivel constantly to catch a fleeting glimpse of a waitstaffer and wave frantically, with a 50 - 50 chance of catching said waitperson's eye.

The food is good, which makes the wait palatable. This frenetic stasis is not done in silence. Voices merge and soar echoically throughout the establishment. So do gasps, grunts, coughs and a fart or two. One may attempt to isolate a random conversation, which invariably deals with aches, pains and diseases unknown to science which afflict the residents.

This is a highly exagerated portrayal of a Twilight Zone mealtime at Riverrun.

TRISDANA

Riverrun is a singularly unique Senior Residence.

The waitstaff in the dining hall are wraiths and ... non-wraiths.*

Riverrun was built upon land purchased from Native Wiccans, (NW) who enriched the land with inner core of their ancestors; burying them there. They became part of the land and were permanent in it. Their ancestral psyches could not be exorcised from the land; they were benign and kept the soil fresh and clean as well.

The NWs, after much deep thought, consulting with the ancestors and balancing their budget, deeded the property and therefor their ancestors over to the new management, Riverrun, which therefor inherited the ancestral souls who consulted amongst themselves and decided that they had enough of dirt and therefor transformed their status and dimension to become dining hall wraiths and ... non-wraiths. Wait staff, that is. The non-wraiths went along with the majority, not really wanting to become waitstaff.

The wraiths took the standard form of waitpersons; humans, but insubstantial, rather like holograms.

The history of the wraiths and ... non-wraiths was told with pomp and ceremony and a video in a tasteful ceremony by the Management to new Residents who might have heard rumors about odd conditions in Riverrun. Persons of the cloth attended new Resident briefings in case there were any religious queries before the new Residents signed their rental contracts.

This was the arrangement: The wraiths accepted and delivered evening meal orders, waft them to the kitchen and tastefully presented their meals to the Resident's for their gustatory delight.

Breakfast and lunch were arranged by the Residents themselves.

The .... non-wraiths clear the tables. The ... non-wraiths were a unique form of the wraiths; those wraiths who could not and would not accept the turnover of the property nor assume human form, but they could not disengage themselves from the area. They would not give themselves a name and so became ...non-wraiths.

A Resident finishes eating, sets down knife, spoon and fork. Plates and tableware are deftly and swiftly whisked away not by the wraiths, but by ... non-wraiths.

The ... non-wraiths manifested themselves as flickers which most of the time impinged on the diner's peripheral vision.

Finally, the ... non-wraith flickerings became a bit much for some residents and a Resident's Investigatory Committee (RIC) was formed to seek a definitive answer as to what the flickerings were because many residents became vertiginous, some fatally, by the whisking flickering who were flickering .... flickering .... flickering.

"WE WANT ANSWERS NOW! WE'RE TIRED OF GETTING FLICKERED!", read the placards carried by those ambulatory Residents. and supported by motorised, vertically challenged, chanting Residents, who plastered their go-carts with placards and popped wheelies in the corridors by the Management offices. The Management caved in.

The management and the RIC could not locate any Native Wiccans to mediate after extensive, expensive investigations. They ascertained that all of the NWs involved in the Riverrun transaction were now on another plane of existence or meditating on mountain peaks. So they paid the investigators grudgingly and called it quits.

By that time, the number of vertiginous Residents had dwindled because of apathy and sheer laziness. Some actually went to meditate with the NWs, some just said the hell with it. Many of the Residents had also dozed off after a pit stop for refreshments and drifted away after awakening. They forgot the issue and adapted themselves to the flickering.

The matter could have been settled then and there in good faith by the Magement and the RIC but for one item.

One of the RIC members, a person of indeterminate age named Dana had fallen in love with a ... non-wraith. It happened in this way:

During an attempt by the RIC to catch a ... non-wraith in the act of whisking, Dana, a member of the RIC had, little by little worked past peripheral vision and saw a ... non-wraith in the act.

Dana thought about and researched the matter long and hard. He had obtained an ecotoplasm trap, which was the nearest he sould come to a ... non-wraith's configuration from an obscure company in Arkham, Massachussetts. Dana modified the apparatus and hoped that it was sensitive enough to capture a ... non-wraith.

It worked!

The ... non-wraith struggled weakly in the trap. Dana extracted the captured one and was immediately, unwillingly translated into a Timelessness Zone where he discerned a shape. He kept the shape from flickering by staring at it and focussed on the name Tristanna in order to retain the ... non-wraith. Tristanna was a long lost love of Dana. Dana kept focus on Tristanna and found that the origin of the name Tristanna was an that of an ancient earth spirit rather than an obstinate soul ancestor of the Native Wiccans. This was a revelation to both Dana and the NWs.

This simplified matters for Dana but royally pissed off the Management and the RIC, who did not know the character of Dana's attraction and already spent way to much non-refundable money trying to locate the elusive NWs. The NWs heard about the situation and sent a representative to Riverrun, which mollified the Management somewhat.

The NWs were kept in the loop then and managed to keep out of the way.

In the Timeless Zone after what seemed a long psyche exchange between Dana and Tristanna, Dana became deeply enamoured of what he perceived as "her". Eons seemed to pass as the pair came to know and love each other. They melded in a ceremony retrieved from archives centuries old.

It was time to end the timelessness. The melded pair snapped out of the Zone. Only a minute had passed in Real Time. The meld was now named Trisdana, who unhesitatingly informed the Management and RIC very carefully of their circumstances. The Management were absolutely confounded.

A compromise was worked out whereby Trisdana would act in a supervisory capacity for the food service, since that was where it all began.

The Management and the residents accepted the situation and resigned themselves to it. The waitstaff wraiths actually cheered just above audible wavelength and served an extra desert to the Residents to show that wraiths were not entirely insensitive.

The unique Trisdana then actually worked up the Riverrun ladder to join corporate headquarters in WinstonSalem NC and became CEO of Riverrun Inc. and head of the Wraith's Union. Health benefits were rather difficult to manage. The other wraiths and ... non-wraiths served and flickered on in Riverrun, unionised.

No other Resident was ever able to entrap a ... non-wraith. Never ever.

RiverRun, Management and Residents existed happily ever after.

*No satisfactory name was found for the ... non-wraiths in English or any Indo-European derived language. The Native Wiccans refered to them by some absolutely untranslatable ineffable cosmic term which could only be formed in the innermost core of the soul. So, the term ... non-wraiths was used hence forward.

DU MER

Lord Aleksandr and Lady Yelena Du Mer are the Sprig of a Branch of the cadet branch of Tsar Alexander Romanov, Emperor of all the Russias and ignorant of them all, which led to his and his family's Empirical exit from terrestrial ken.

This is pertinent here because the Sprig saw the Cyrillic writing on the wall (they spoke only French, considering their native Russian *infra dig,* fit only for proletrians and workers of the world). After translation of Mene Mene Tekel Upharsin as "the writing on the wall", meaning a very negative connotation, they hauled ass, bag and baggage and several dozen gold bars out of the Winter Palace to refuge in Smögasbroad, capital of Stanisstan, a long way from home.

There they established a dynasty, determined not to die nasty, as their relatives did. They mixed and mingled with the well bread upper crust of the Stanisstanians, creating the distinguished, among other epithets, couple that we know fondly as "Lord Aleksandr and Lady Yelena Du Mer".

That should serve as a brief history of the Lordly couple, a curtailed resumé of thousands of years of Viking Rus history and mythology.

They were an imposing pair: Aleksandr, a tall, stereotypical heir of the Romanovs (no matter how far removed), being just shy of 6 nogi 7 dyumov, goateeed (the extra 'e' because an Atlas Mountain Ram supplied the hair), muscled like an eight pack of beer, an extrovert of stentorian speech capable of being heard many versts away and scaring infants, a visage that of Alexander the Great. Altogether, a gentile giant.

Yelena, Al's fifth cousin once removed (to Siberia), a few

dyuymov shorter, was a curvaceous, armed (9 mm Glöck) Venus de Milo, softly spoken but with a voice capable of piercing ears half a verst away.

The LA and LY love match had several offspring who had sprung off immediatly upon reaching their majority, which in Stanisstan meant as soon as they accumulated 10 Stanisstanian Capeks. The least spoken of them, the better. Besides, they have no immediate impact upon the principals in this saga.

They were owned by a magnificent Borzoi, Rooshian Wolf Hound) who was obsessed with scaring and devouring Cossacks who ventured near the Du Mer's modest castle in Stanisstan. Boris the Borzoi sometimes mistook the mailman for a Cossack. This caused a large turnover in postmen, an avoidance of the route to the modest castle.

Postmen took to leaving the mail (99.9% bills) with the neighbor, who lived a number of versts away and was rather reluctant to deliver the mail to the Du Mers because of Boris. So the neighbor, a clever sort of chap, fashioned a magnificent suit of armour and thusly delivered the bills. He was outstanding in his field as a substitue mail carrier and was held in high regard by his peers. One day he was out standing in his field. It rained, and he became the most rusted knight in the area. Pardon the digression.

The imposing couple, as characterised previously, decided to go bungee jumping one fine day at Bannergee, Chattergee and Mukergee's Indian Curry and Bungee Starbuck's. They were experienced jumpers, having bungeed all across their route of escape from Mama Rooshia, leaping but not bouncing back across Sea, Land and Air (pockets), earning the sobriquet of The Du Mer SEALS. To stretch a point, they made it to Stanisstan with the aid of a flexible Slav called the Rubber Czech who defrauded banks for travel funds for the Du Mers. The gold bars turned out to be gold (24 carats) plated lead bars. The (dirty) dozen Romanov serfs who helped the Du Mers to escape were no dummies. They skipped town with the real things and opened a Russian Tea Room in Coney Island, Brooklyn and financed the Russian Mafia. Pardon the digression.

So, attaching and being attached to the cords, they leaped from a very high bridge (named after Chester Molar, DDS). The spectators - the families of Bannergee, Chattergee and Mukergee - viewed them as they bounded and rebounded under the bridge.

Somehow intuitively anticipating an unexpected turn of events, knowing the Du Mers, the Bs, Cs and Ms, along with a few unemployed loitering Stanisstanians, scrambled off the bridge and disappeared down the mountainside like kangaroos. (a rarity in Stanisstan). They were followed by Boris. He was hungry.

The unexpected manoeuver was performed, which resulted in the couple (they were coupled together) looped over the bridge, spinning centripetally, released their bungee couplings and arrowed straight for their modest castle by personal jetpacks which were concealed under their ermine cloaks. They landed in the interior patio in the koi pond, a slight divergence from their flight plan. The dispaced koi were not pleased but were rescued by Zany (as Aleksandr called himself). After hauling Yellie (as Yelena nicknamed herself) from the pond, he deposited the displaced koi, who koyly dived to the depths af the pond and koypulated in relief. Pardon the digression.

Lord and Lady divested their bungee gear and donning evening ermines, each sipping from individual white Rooshians, lounged in their lounge chairs. chasing away a couple of lounge lizards, and contemplated the sunset over the Stanisstanian peaks.

Boris the Borzoi lounged at their feet, repleted, nay, sated, with a few pounds of pseudo-Sanisstanians made of gelatin, which tasted a lot better than the real thing. The real things clothing were indigestible, causing a very exotic deposit by Boris in delicate areas.

"A day vell shpent, dunt you tink?" they declared together in English, one of the many languages they spoke accentlessly and perfectly.

Who knows what further adventures may befoul Lord Zany and Lady Yellie? Stay tuned.

FOUR CORNERS

During 1951-52, I traveled across the 38th parallel in Frozen Chosen from east to west and back again as an infantry radio operator.

As we zig-zagged our way across the peninsula, the guys in our platoon knew what they wanted to do when they got back Stateside, Nothing incoming except mail, eat, sleep, alone or otherwise, enjoying family life. Me too, with one difference.

I wanted to stand on a street corner in the West Bronx. Just stand there.

I do not know why. I still do not know why after sixty seven years.

I got back to the Bronx in July 1952. I took an IRT subway to the last stop, Moshulu Pkwy.

I stood on each of the four corners in turn and looked around and at the buildings. Up. Down. Sideways. I sniffed, coughed. I searched the sky. No UFOs. NOTHING. Not a vibration, not an epiphany. Just the midday sun. Not even a person walking by or entering or leaving one of the buildings.

I went back to the East Bronx. Home.

Whence the obsession? I never lived in the neighborhood in which I was standing. I knew no one who lived there.

We were being nostalgic on one occasion, my wife and I, chatting about people and places we'd been when I had a flashback to my Bronx corner journey. I told this to my wife who immediately scoffed at the whole account. I was completely gormless, dozy and daft, she opined. She dismissed it entirely. No speculation. Nothing further. Period.

No, I do NOT think of this constantly. It was a flashback. It is NEITHER my "raison d'etre" NOR my obsession.

"Go ahead, go back to the Bronx - or the Army!", (We were in Virginia.) She scoffed. She scoffs very well. And gets quite irritated, too. She's right, y'know.

For a moment I was tempted Bronx wise. Reason prevailed. Let the Four Corners go, man, go. Get a life.

N.B. I will give my name, rank, serial number and any other information deemed relevant to my "Raison d'etre" = obsession if you can figure this bit out. Be a shrink. Enjoy.

FUNKING AROUND

I was standing at a window in Troop Command Headquarters (TCU), lightly sweating in the hot orderly room (OR), thumbs hitched in the belt loops of my Battle Dress Uniform (BDU), staring at the empty company street. The company clerk paid me no attention. squinting at various Field Manuals (FMs) in the harsh light of a 100 Watt bulb (BULB).

A sudden summer storm hissed its cargo of rain against the grimy panes, just after I returned from jeeping around the company area accomplishing my mission: the welfare of my troops. A Government Issue (GI) would have to degrime those windows ASAP!

Static I stood, inside listening to the outside bitching and moaning of the storm. I was in a funk between blue and feeling-sorry-for-myself because I was a lifer here at Fort Zinderneuf, my last hitch before I faded away; hanging up my dress blues with all the chest candy indicating that I was almost a hero and got shot at and missed and shit at and hit.

Grimy panes to grimy mirrors. The only place in barracks where there are mirrors is in the latrines. That's just to see if your head is still attached to your body, you can recognize yourself and you have made a supreme effort to shave. Otherwise, your squad leader or platoon sergeant can comment on your state of military preparedness in order to acquit yourself tactical-wise-uniform-wise. There's your grimy pain in the dress-right-dress.

My troops were in the field funking around on maneuvers, wetter inside than out, for that is the nature of US Army wet weather gear. Water will find its level. No sissy crap like umbrellas. Damn, the Defense Advanced Research Projects

Agency (DARPA), could come up with a multi-purpose rifle/ umbrella that'd shoot and keep the troops dry at the same time. Only the Bulgarians used devices like that – a hypodermic needle umbrella, yet! Sly Slavic suckers!

My troops would be sniffling in tomorrow on sick call. Upper respiratory tract infections, they'd tell me, shit-house medics all. The company clerk would fill out DD Form 689, Individual Sick Slip and check off "illness in the line of duty". Sick call – the morning parade of the sick, lame and lazy, blind deaf and crazy. They should all be robots. Or androids, better, Shades of Karel Kapek and Rabbi Jehuda Loew. No sick call. No mail call. No chow. Army chow isn't very lethal; it just tastes like that. But all those androids could march perfectly in review. Dress right dress, count cadence count. TC 3-21-5 (Army Study Guide) or FM 21-18 (Drill and Ceremonies). Not like my flesh and blood troopies here at Fort Zinderneuf who'd be sure to shout out of cadence. Although we simply cannot fight in a participatory war without the human element. It just wouldn't be. . . human!

Bulgarians and rain; not such strange bedfellows. It rains in Bulgaria, often at bedtime. Bed was something that I could live with. Even at 0 dark 30. I once watched a pair of Bulgarians, a young pretty miss and an old man, bedecked in their national costumes, The old man carried the pretty miss halfway through - shuffle through a bed of glowing coals during a …. but that's another story, another mission.

Back to bed. I was suddenly infatuated with that summery showery moment outside with bed. I was tired mentally, physically and funkally with the assininity of it all, especially TC. My troops. I was Momma and Poppa to them. Adults with pre-Bar Mitsvah minds, Adofuckinglescents. My troops with their late 20th century bright shiny illusions colliding with my early 20th century illusions, shattered and stuck together with instant superglue. A crazed reflecting surface. Crazy illusory shadows.

The multiplex of fatuation. Permutations and combinations of fatuation.

What kind of fatuation fall I prey to? Unrequited love kind? Why not requited; be mutually fatuated. Am I seekng mutual fatuation? YesNo. Ambivalence: Why? Hurt? Fatuated and fatuatee and vice versa. How does a fatuate feel? I squeak for myself only. Frustrated – angry – distanced in infinite sadness. Afraid of overfatuation? Antifatuated. Why? Among other things, infatuation to me is tactile. I am not very tactile. When I get tactile, I am really tactile. Enter she. She's tactile. With her, tactility conveys a more complete communication. Which may be misinterpreted. Do I want to get outinfatuatedtactily. How about them tactics? There's a touching story in there somewhere.

Maybe the object of my infatuation is subtly body-languaging me that I am not the subject of her interest. Doesn't want to wound me. "I don't want to wound you, Top. It's not you. it's me!" Yeah, see you around. Not a Purple Heart for my dress blues. Just a near miss. I miss that Miss. A set of dress blues isn't cheap. I can buy a firewalking Bulgarian complete with hypodermic rifle umbrella for less than the price of a set of dress blues. I am only squeaking for myself. What a mindblast.

What is the trajectory of an infatuation? Can it be plotted like that of an artillery round? (See one of many FMs. Start with FM 6-20-1J, Field Artillery.) Artillery can supply indirect fire. I am the indirect forward observer of my own trajectory. I inform Fire Direction Control (FDC) of the shell's impact on the enemy. A shell of my former self. An arc through the sky. Slamming through sudden-shower-making clouds. Shower shadows inside and out. A parade of shadows. Never rains in the Army – rains on the Army. A subtle military distinction covering a wet weather gear, incipient pneumonia and a multitude of other sins. Firewalking shadows from here to infinity.

Still raining. Still standing here in timeless minutes. For some fraction of real world time I am here. Feeling like a flickering TV (television) screen TV reception here at Fort Zinderneuf is not of the best, surrounded as we are by mountainous sand dunes. So we watch X-rated cassettes. Off-duty, of course. On-duty has its own X-rated moments. The human body can be bent and twisted Kama Sutra-wise in so many positions, especially when entwined with another(s). Maybe they are androids?

I once invited the object of my infatuation to the profane military oasis of Ft. Zinderneuf to experience the irreality of military time. She wisely declined. I have had no visitors. I finally decide that I want no visitors, being non-tactile.

Oddly enough, there's a two year gap in the military trajectory of my memory. I remember being attached to an artillery outfit and that is it. Must have been traumatic. Too many big booms? Is that another story?

Ah, raining juring duty hours. Fragmented between grimy windowpanes and fantasy and instant superglued illusions of reality. Alone in a crowd, Alone in the NCO club lipping a beer, listening to ol' soldiers and wannabe ol' soldiers swapping bullshit. This ol' Top did the mandatory 4 mile walk/run in 50 minutes 49 seconds and I had 80 minutes to do it in! That meant that I can keep re-enlisting, embracing our state of nowar nopeace preparing for noworld. What would a 50min 49sec lifer do on M-Day (Mobilization)? Teach the troopies how to be infantry sojers from my accumulated wisdom IAW (In Accordance With) Army Regulation (AR) 611-201, Enlisted Career Management Field (EMF) and Military Occupational

Speciality (MOS), CMF 11, Infantryman. MOS 11B states '... closes with and destroys enemy personnel, weapons and equipment." MOS11B10 through 11B50 each delegate a more specialized enemy-destroying function. Go read the AR. Every farshlugginer MOS in the Army is detailed.

The Infantry has no civilian equivalent in the Dictionary of Occupational Titles (DoT). No Federal Civil Service Classification equivalent. Imagine us, trained to be steely-eyed, iron-gutted killers, let loose on society. Read all 1,000 pages. A barrel of laughs. I'll train 'em, allowed to stand funkally, dryly immersed in a rainstorm. I will leave the NCO club half pissed and get lost. Show me the way to go home,

Barracks, temporary since maybe 1941, are numbered on one side only, so that some feckless wight taken in drink must stagger around three sides of a rectangle to distinguish one clone from another, as if he/she/it remembers some feature of the clone. The rationale of army barracks is fulsomely detailed in AD-A266-690, US CERL Technical Report CRC-93 01, Army Corps of Engineers. No reason can be discerned for the numbering of the structures. The Bulgarians number their buildings on all four sides. Sly Slavic buggers!

Bulgarians, shadows and funks. My unreal reality. Where is it..........

"Hey Top," the company clerk shattered my bit and pieces to smaller bits and pieces.

"The Cap'n wants ya."

The Railroad Tracks! I gotta grab the 'phone and hustle my ass. In wet weather gear I must hustle. Since we NCOs run the Army, I might as well wander over and see how Cap and I can advance democracy.

Peace be with you.

Top, who salutes you.

THE HERO

A terrible fire was burning furiously, smoke and embers everywhere. People could be heard screaming inside the building.

A man went running into the inferno, heedless of his own safety and emerged, half-carrying, half dragging two people with him.

The fire truck and an ambulance arrived seconds after the alarm had be sounded and immediately set about controling the blaze. It was brought under control in two hours.

A reporter spotted and questioned the man who had saved the lives of two people before he slipped away.

"Sir, you are a hero, you know, to do what you did with no asssurance that you were going to survive is truly a heroic act. Why did you do this?

The man blushed and replied, "I am a recovering coward. I fell off the wagon!"

A FAIR EXCHANGE

"You know," said Lady Yellie, "the exchange rate is 8,000 Kapocs to one US Dollar. That should bring the tourists flocking here to Stanisstan."

"Yes, sweet thang," replied Lord Zany, the tourists may split a lip smiling at the rate and think that they are getting a tremendous bargain. Remember, it costs 8,000 Ks for cup of coffee."

"Darn", frowned Lady Yellie. sipping her shandy, followed by an Arnold Palmer and a scrumpy, "I forgot."

"Keep drinking those liquid bombshells and you'll be exchanging a lot of Kapocs for dollars to get your stomach pumped in the Dlanodpmurt hospital cum mortuary right quick.

"Zany - I really don't think any more that fooling around with the Kapoc is worth the trouble. We'll just get caught in the money market fluctuations and keep getting flucked. Let's do something cool with the gold we scraped off the lead bars those momsers scammed us with. They scammed us, but coated the lead with so much gold to fool us, that we actually scraped off a whole bunch of money, so they got scammed."

"OK, Yellie, cast the pale shadow of your thought over a cool caper."

"OK. here's an idea: let's buzz the capitol building in Smorgasbroad and toss out leaflets praising Stashiu lll and recounting all the things he has done for his country. Actually, the old rogue has done Stanisstan a great deal of good. Hey, also toss out 8,000 Kapoc notes overprinted with 'Have a cuppa coffee on me! Courtesy your People's President (for life) Stashiu lll!' ".

"Yeah," said Zany," I gotta admit he has done a lot of good, especially by granting us asylum.

"Ah, C'mon, you actually like the old bugger; he didn't have you drawn and quartered even when you gave him the exploding cigar and he sat on the whoopie cushion," she giggled.

"Well, it put holes in his favorite bow tie and he didn't think farts were that funny, but I convinced him that he could do the same thing to his Minister of Divertissments, the scowlpus old bastard. I think that he did and got a charge out of it. I saw the MoD with his goatee cut real short though."

"OK, let's get the heli ready, leaflets printed and Kapocs overprinted. Gotta be in and out like a monk in a nunnery or else we'll get shot down for entering prohibited space." proclaimed Yellie.

"That radar I sold him has a 34 1/2 second delay, so we got plenty of time." pronounced Zany.

Off went the pair, parachutes on backs and fortified with their civic betterment goals.

They approached the restricted zone and prepared to air drop their cargo. The 34 1/2 second delay had passed by one nanosecond when a cloud of what appeared to be balloons filled with a substance arched over the helicopter and burst, several by the open doors of the heli, showering the aircraft and occupants with a foul smelling substance identified by the drenched couple as enhanced horse manure.

"Holy shit, I didn't know that Stashu lll had it in him to think of that," Zany spluttered, struggling to hold the craft steady as it exited the restricted zone with one hand, clearing his goggles with another, holding his nose at the same time and suddenly realizing that he didn't have three hands.

"What a hell of a way to discourage intruders. Stink 'em away, or let them land in that hill of crap I saw just before we got out of range of the shit storm" spat Yellie.

"Well, we spread our load anyway," said Zany. "And in spite of the fact that we'll smell olf enhanced horse manure, unless we get ourselves to the jet spray right quick, I can't help but admire the old fart's ingenuity. And I can't get really angry. Let's hustle or he'll have his stink hounds unleashed and trace us down."

So, off they sped to their hangar and indulged is a great spray party, stripping off their clothes and hosing each other off of the enhanced horse manure with a good deal of horsing around themselves. Much fun with, "Neigh, neigh, sirrah remove thy hands from my fetlocks or I shall geld thee."

"Ah, would'st thou, fair sidesaddle rider," grinned Zany, "I wouldst curry comb thy tail, maid; do not turn around too fast, pray. Think of the consequences."

And so it went, each galloping a furlong or two to reach the finish line - a photo finish, with some interesting photos snapped.

They retired to their beach side lounges, each sipping an enhanced Arnold Palmer.

Another day, another Kapoc, they sighed in unison, as the President's stink hounds barked past and vanishing into the fields and woods, frightening a few partying peasants silly and eating up their picnics with pleasure and abandon.

MOMMASAN

My sister calls her "Mom". I've called her "Mommasan" since I came back from Korea in the summer of 1953.

In the Blumenthal Home in Clemmons, NC, where she lived, she was known as "Teddy", short for Teresa.

My two wife, two sons, sister and brother-in-law and I celebrated her 98th birthday in August, 2000 along with the nursing staff, who baked her a cake.

Until a couple of years ago she recognized us, my sister and her husband more than my crowd, since she lived in Raleigh, NC and we lived in Virginia Beach. Then she began to drift into the past, the present for her was now dream like. She remembered her WWI sailor husband, her life in Manhattan in the 'twenties and her life as a flapper, not that she flapped that much. Mommasan told us about her three sisters, all of whom had passed on, two of whom, including Mommasan, had been born in some village near Kiev.

Then she began to create a past, one which we knew didn't exist; she became a school teacher who taught her students how to make stuffed cabbage, borscht and schav. She was promoted to headmistress. We listened to her recipies.

Mommasan began treating us like kindly visiting strangers, able to laugh with us and thanking us kindly for visiting with her.

We mourned her confusion of time and space and the loss of our identities to her. We were happy that she still responded to our conversational sallies with some sense. We respected her anchor in the past and filtered the now.

The last time we visited her, realizing that that time might well be the last, her nurse brought her into the common room in her mechanical marvel of a reclining chair. We made small talk as usual, simply not willing to relinquish her entirely to the end. I put my thumb to my nose and wiggled my fingers, a gesture I used once in a while to evince a giggle. Then I took her hands in mine. She smiled and said something which filled me with an inexpressible emotion.

"You are a nice man," her grip tightend a fraction. "I would like you to meet my son Stanley. he calls me 'Mommasan'

RIVERRUN

RiverRun Independent Senior Structure, physical plant and residents, has had many incarnations in these scribblings.

Familiarity with the theme may have dulled the edge of anticipation for readers, but RiverRun presents itself in so many facets to me (**436**) that it is difficult to stray from within the framework. So please consider each anecdote on its own merit.

Feel free to comment on each mini-saga.

Included are other musings, equally commentable upon.

Be Aware. There is no sex here!

SHIFT

Did you ever wake up, go through your morning routine, go to breakfast, and really think that you were in another dimension?

From my present status as a single, happy resident of a condo. There is a bit of a turnover of tenants which means that there are new faces from time to time, so that an unfamiliar face isn't all that uncommon.

But one does become accustomed to the features and other characteristics of one's tablemates. Lunch and dinner in the main building is a nice touch; the food is good. But we do tend to sit with the same clique for breakfast. Lunching and dinnering together is less frequent; tends to be with other residents, so any seeming differences in population is not so apparent.

During the breakfast on this day the faces and characteristics of the three men opposite me were subtly not the same as yesterday. Were faces shifted somehow? Not radically. Just enough so that there it appeared to me that there were three dopplegangers across the table from me. The faces and the people attached to them regarded me with the same acceptance as always, I thought. Or did they? Was there a knowing expression on their faces knowing that they knew that I knew that they weren't the same as yesterday?

We did engage in the normal conversational gambits, "Good morning," "How goes it?" "How wags the world with thee?" I said to each of my tablemates.

And the normal responses, "What's so good about it?" "Too early to tell," and "Huh?"

Maybe I just didn't really *look* at each person when I sat down to crunch my bowl of grain flakes and down a half cup of coffee and a scone. Or they didn't really hear me and I didn't hear their routine responses. Propinquity breeds subconcious acceptance? Or something? That was possible.

It was also possible that I was entering the first stage of hallucinatory dementia. I don't remember what I really saw when looked in the bathroom mirror. Would I recognize any shifting anythings in my face? Or body?

I tried to examine each face unobtrusively. There were changes, I swear. One breakfaster was drinking orange juice instead of prune juice. The other was drinking some colored fluid instead of iced tea.

Well, so what? A change of beverage?

One got up to leave. He had a slight limp, which he never exhibited before. Again, so what? maybe he tripped or something? A second man left the table. He looked alright ...... except for a small mole on his righht cheek, which I swear wasn't there before!

Ah, c'mon! I didn't sleep well last night. The roast thing I had for dinner wasn't cooked well. A touch of indigestion, 'sall! I was just experiencing a brain fart.

I left before the third breakfaster left the table. He looked startled for a moment. Wasn't I supposed to leave yet? Hoo boy! Nut house here I come.

The lobby looked about the same; the chairs were rearranged for each event, so that was no guage of any differences or dimension shift. The desk chap looked OK. Or, wait a minute - what color was his hair? NUTS!

I went outside to look aroud and check the temperature. Nice weather. I looked up.

There was only one sun in the sky.

J-38

Ah, Korea. Frozen Chosen.

From the Yellow Sea we moved West on the Korean peninsula to the Sea of Japan in the East: that is, from Inch'on to Yongdungp'o to the Iron Triangle of Pyonggang to Ch'or won to Kumhwa to what we called the Punchbowl, the South Koreans called Haen Yanggu to Paekto/Whitehorse/Papasan/Kaesong on the Sea of Japan and back again. We kept every site on the map stitched together with J-38s!

In our line company's universe, riding on the CW through my headphones I tapped out in Morse on my J-38 - "dit dit dit daah, dit dit daah, dit dit dit daah", which are the opening bars of Beethoven's Fifth and also "Victor" in the phonetic alaphabet. I completed the net call, which was received 5 X 5 and acknowledged. Our phonetic alphabet was "Able: dit dah, Baker: dit dit dit daah, Charlie: daah dit dah dit, Dog: daah dit dit ..." Come see me and I'll key it out for you.

But in my universe ....

When I say, "In my universe", I guess that was the begining of me going "dit happy". Nothing but the omnipresent cosmic static, day or night in my 'phones. Different at night when every radio transmission gets bounced around by some phenomenon in the sky; a "skip wave".

We mastered Morse code, not the composition of the earth's atmosphere. All those layers never seemed to bother the CW, the Continuous Wave with which we stitched together the peninsula, dit by daah.

Yeah, me and my universe. An Intermediate Speed Radio

Operator, MOS 1740. I also carried the indestructible MI Garand.

What I listened to was a symphony of hisses and crackles and almost decipherable and understandable speech which stayed in my head. A regular siren song, it was. A song of the spheres; music of the spheres!

What came to me and stayed was a melody; no lyrics, a wordless song in my universe which wafted in and out of my 'phones. It slid under and over all my transmissions. It was eerily beautiful.

And then, one shift, there were words to the song. Indecipherable lyrics, but sounds, words, maybe, on the very verge of being understandable. No earthly language? I actually began hearing the melody off shift. I realized that this wasn't right. I asked my buddies if they heard anything other than the regular background static and radio chatter? No, but one of 'em was a Hawaiian of Japanese descent and said that once in a while he could hear a Japanese taxi driver talking. Other than that, nothing.

I just didn't want the rest of the squad to think what l was afraid that they might think - like trying to get a Section Eight discharge - a nut case.

I'm told that I did get an Honorable Discharge under a legitimate Section 8. I just don't remember the circumstances under which it happened. Anyway....

Anyway, listen, Sarge, thanks for listening, sorry, but I gotta get my J-38. I can really get that waveband now and listen real good with my 'phones and figure out what she is singing and write it down. See ya soon, Sarge. He saluted.

I returned his salute, I heard his story many times now. He can call me Sarge. I went to my office. I entered my notes and his notes in his file. His notes looked like scribbles, legible to him only. I once asked him to read them to me. He did. In no

Earthly language. And he didn't seem to notice that I didn't understand. I'm sure that someone, someday, would translate them into an Earthly language. I'd like to be around for that.

It's good that I let one of my aides put his story on the web. Maybe somebody will recognize him. No kin is on file. No anybody is on file. He was brought here from the NYPD 14th Precinct at 2 East 169th St., The Bronx.

How he got to the 14th Precinct is still a mystery.

His military records indicate that he was in the commo platoon, HQ and HQ Co., 14th Inf. Regt., 25th Div., 8th Army from '51 -'53. He fell off the radar from his discharge until now.

Was it a coincidence, him appearing at the14th? The cops ran a check on him and put out a Missing Person bulletin. "Caucasian, 5'6", 30 years old. Black hair, brown eyes, fair complexion. No facial hair. No distinguishable bodily markings".

Nothing, more nothing. A nibble or two. When followed through, false alarm. You'd figure that at least one of his old buddies would have contacted him. But, no! Why? Some good Samaritan picked up on the web story and, in a grand anonymous gesture, bailed him out of a holding cell and sent him to us.

He wafts in and out of "dit happy". Transmits net calls to his line companies on the hour. Listens, replies and then seems to fade into his headphones. The music and lyrics of his spheres; his universe, no doubt.

My name is Ioséfus Ivanovich Syenovitcii, PhD, MD. They call me "JoeSen".

THE LOST "T" AND GRANDMOTHER

"ICED TEA?? THE VERY WORD IS ANETHEMA TO ME! I WANT NO 'ICED TEA' NEAR ME OR MINE!!! AND YOUR 'HOT TEA', IF I MAY USE THAT TERM WITHOUT GAGGING, IS NOTHING BUT TINTED, TEPID WATER. exclaimed my Grandmother in her best CAPITAL LETTER QUEEN'S ENGLISH.

NO, I WILL **NOT** KEEP MY KNIFE! THERE MUST BE A TERRIBLE SHORTAGE OF KNIVES IN THIS COUNTRY!"

Receiving this barrage of CAPITALS, the waiter immediately backed off as if my Grandmother's CAPITALS were steel pointed crossbow bolts targeted directly at his hapless body. He moved backwards until he hit the wall and attempted to merge into it to the adjoining room. He might have tried for the skylight If he hadn't been impaled by superbly enunciated CAPITAL LETTERS. His towel, embroided with the legend "Restaurant Le Bon Momsér, draped over his arm, proved no shield to my Grandmother's righteous bolts of verbiage.

"I aplogize, Madam, I'm truly sorry, I ..." the waiter stuttered, regaining his professional mein, not succeeding in merging into the wall. He prayed his that years of serving all sorts of international entities would surge from his soul and come to mind and help him handle this particular entity.

"I AM NOT 'MADAM'! I AM LADY HERMIONE BARRINGTON-SMYTHE, MY GOOD MAN", Lady

Barrington-Smythe aimed her QUEEN'S ENGLISH at the unravelled server.

She started anew in lower case, having put the waiter in his place. Not unkindly, she regarded him, Albert Theélder, as his name plate indicated and spoke. "Ah, you colonials."

"UMM! Albert vocalized. His embroidered towel and years of service could did not aid him in his time of need. He merged into the next room and tendered his resignation, taking the towel with him. He later surfaced at Malatesta's Kosher Kitchen, towel and all.

It was a very good thing that we were in a private room of "Le Bon Momsér" in SoHo, New York, which Lady Barrington-Smythe had chosen because the name appealed to her and her cousin owned it.

There were no other diners in our select spot to embarrass us. This was a reserved room, after all.

The manager, known to the other patrons as M'sieu André and to me as Uncle Moishe, was present for the exchange, semi-hidden behind a faux Corinthian column. He approached our table with the soundless glide of a restauranteur of the first class.

He learned and perfected this soundless glide from avoiding spilled two-cents plain and various confections in his candy store on Freeman St. in The Bronx. He built it up from a former cigar maker's shop, after receiving a decent sum as reparations from Deutschland as a Holocaust survivor. Money could not erase every memory. He wore long sleeves. "Ruchel, it's me, calm down. I'll fix it. Have some English breakfast tea".

Allow me an aside here: Lady Hermione was my grandmother because her sister's branch of the family had made it to England just before Jewish life in Europe was practically extinguished. She and two brothers had some English language lessons courtesy of an ex-pat Brit. They did have a natural aptitude for languages, which helped. Also, I'm really not sure of family relationships; to whom am I blood-related to? Maybe I was adopted? A lot of confusion after WWII.

My mother was her daughter Sara, emigrated to the US in the 1900s. Mom and dad passed away some years ago. I am their only child.

To continue: This was Lady Hermione's first visit to the US. They shot roots in England and mourned all of their relative who didn't make it out. They'd show the bastards that they survived!! Their ex-pat British tutor gave them an idea about the British upper clahss. The Book!

Diligent research in Brett's peerage lead them to assuming the identities of a presumed extinct line of Barrington-Smythes. Ruchel Sara became Hermionie Phillipa Barrington-Smythe; her two brothers, Reginald and Percival B-S. Time, however, had finally claimed for itself Reginald and and Percival, leaving Hermione to carry on the line. Hermione never married.

The trio succeeded beyond their wildest dreams in actually inheriting a manor house in Yorkshire and becoming more British than the British.

I had invited Grandma over to America because she wanted me to inherit their manor house.

So endeth the aside.

I was born in The Bronx, USA because my parents were a not-so-distant branch of the original Berkovic/wich/ line who made it here before WWII. That's another story courtesy of the Wandering Jew.

"Ruchel, schvester, this is Moishe you're talking to. Calm down and we'll get you a gluzzel tea and a shtick shugar."

"Moishe," She said, "First, please stop with the fractured Yiddish! I'm Lady Hermione Barrington-Smythe to you and everyone now." She still had her British accent, which is the way she had learned to speak English in the first place. "Forget the shtetl. Remember Yorkshire!"

"But I am here and I will be here until I talk some sense into Stanley here."

Meanwhile, she was sipping appreciatively from the gluzzel tea.

"OK", I said, "I am unmarried, twenny one and ----"

""STANLEY! YOU FORGOT SOMETHING!"

"What? What?"

"THERE'S A 'T' IN TWENTY-ONE"

"Oy! OK, I'm twenTy one, unmarried and ..."

Grandmother was so sincere that she powered down and spoke in lower case. "Why? A nice Jewish boy like you, a good living, don't smoke, drink...."

"Grandmother, I'm working on it." (No one would dare call her Granma or any variation.)

"Who? I must meet her."

"OK, OK, you will, yes ma'm. Please let's talk about Yorkshire. You know that I really love that place when I stayed there last year. By the way, did anyone ever have any questions about your occupancy of the manor or title?"

"No, Stanley, you Doubting Thomas, with the way that records were destroyed during the war and the willingness of the local lads to put in a days work for the good wages that we were paying for the restoration of the manor house, no questions were asked. In fact, they forgave the occasional slips we made in certain areas such as genealogy as caused by wartime stress and strain."

"Why do you want me as your heir apparent? tell me again. please., Grandmother."

"After researching what remained of our tribe and contacting one or two possibilities, you were selected as the best choice to carry on the line."

"Yeah, and forget the Berkovic/wich, huh"

"Bubbaleh, what's in a name?"

Maybe there was nothing in a name, but they did decide that they must keep their Judaism and so an ingenious plan was hatched.

It is well known tha 'only mad dogs and Englishmen go out in the mid-day sun'. The male line of the original Barrington Smythes had been in India during the Raj and experienced a bit much of the midday sun. After a session or two of Doolally Tap* they claimed affiliation with Werbeh, an offshoot of an interpretation of a Sanskrit mantra and performed the religious rituals which the worship of Werbeh required.

With the credentials of DooLaLi Tap in their CV, they could perform any rituals consonant with Werbeh with impunity, no interference and maintain their B.S. cover. And so they did; even made a conversion or two of the locals.

Grandmother finally convinced me to take an exploratory trip to the Yorkshire manse, all expenses paid. She even had a few JEPs (Jewish English Princesses) lined up for me, which I sort of appreciated.

When Stanley looked in the mirror. he saw a rather out-of-shape twenty year old, 5'9", in need of his black hair being cut, nondescript blue shirt, no tie, black creased trousers. Considering everything, a pleasant face, prone to look as if had just committed a minor gaffe, brown eyes, unclipt eyebrows, just a nose, thin lips. Every woman's man. He snickered and gave himself the finger as he turned away from the unflattering image in the reflection. He had once wondered why he couldn't shake hands with his reflection, tried in the mirror, then gave it up as undoable ... yet.

"Let's see", I said, reverting to the first person singular, "How does one become an Englishman? Vocabulary? Clothes? Body language? Table manners?"

"Vocabulary? Nah, I can't fake an English accent. They know that I'm a Yank. Maybe some expressions, like 'Pipe the haggis', 'toss the cabbie'. Nah. That's Scots.

Body language? I read somewhere that some profiler can tell where a person is from the way he walks. Maybe I should just stride purposefully around the quad?

I'll give it my best and just become Lord Pisher, to the manor born,"

"Stanley, dollink, please don't take too long. The window of opportunity might snap shut before you know it," declared Grandmother.

But, after much thought and study of the English personality, even the DooLally Tap. I decided not to accept Grandmother's offer. I just could not see myself as 'to the manor born' with all the panoply that came along with the title and the property. Werbeh as a religion did not appeal to me, as I thought of myself as a recovering agnostic. I must decline the exploratory trip to Yorkshire and the JEPs, I thought, regreting the lost JEPs. I jetted back to the States

Now, how to break the news to Grandmother, whom I truly adored?

For once in my life, I, Stanley, decided to confront Grandmother with the truth! I girded my loins with a lox, cream cheese and bagel lunch and a two-cents plain. I dialed her number and asked to speak to Grandmother in her apartment on Webster Avenue in the West Bronx.

"Grandmother," I managed to sound less squeaky than I felt, but came right out with it,

"I don't want to go to England. I'll never make - or fake it. I thought about this long and hard."

"AH HA! I THOUGHT THAT YOU WEREN'T AS KEEN AS I THOUGHT. YOU DISAPPOINT ME, BUT, I DID A LITTLE DUE DILIGENCE AND DISCOVERED

THAT MOISHE, OR RATHER M'SIEU ANDRE, WAS REALLY KEEN TO GO. HE'S OLDER AND A MUCH BETTER LIAR - AH, DIPLOMAT - THAN YOU'LL EVER BE,' Grandmother capitalised at me.

She relented and lower-cased. "Nu, you'll still get an allowance every month."

I was a teacher of cursive writing to private students, since the public schools stopped teaching it. I really needed that allowance. It was rather difficult to teach when most of my class was texting. Sometimes I was studentless for a long time. I would otherwise subsist on stale bagels and Orange Julius.

What other career was there for a teacher of cursive handwriting? I do have beautiful cursive, I must admit. People love to get my letters. Only emails! At least I own a computer. Except for cursive, I mostly inhabit the 21st century. My computer trouble shooter must be at least thirteen years old.

"Thank you for the allowance, Grandmother. Y'know, I had a feeling that all this was a setup. I knew that I was right when Uncle Moishe took me aside and said that he actually wanted the Manor in Old Blighty but you talked him into letting me have a first shot at it because you knew that I'd finally say no, but I was a favorite of yours. You had this eleborate charade all figured out, didn't you?!"

"Well..." interrupted Grandmother "I..."

I shall hark back to the 'phone conversation. "Lemme finish." l actually told my Grandmother to shut up, in so many words! "Uncle M. and you are really great actors. You had me fooled from the get go. I must be the most naive person in the world. Grandmother, was the bit about the silverware and the "lost Ts" for real?"

"Yes, it was real There does seem to be a remarkable shortage of knives in the US. So, my somewhat favorite naive nephew, you may go with my for-real-matriarchal-blessings, and sin no more."

So, I went. Susequent communications from Uncle Moishe from Old Blighty indicated that he got along right well with the folks there. He had to squelch the rumour that he had been awarded the Victoria Cross because that was going a bit too far in his role as a Barrington Smythe. He did have a moral sense, it seemed and a lovely JEP who enjoyed his company, he Skyped.

He was, in fact, enjoying himself far more that I ever could; Uncle M's years as maitre d' and schmoozer serving him well.

I married a former student of mine, who had all sorts of cursives in the right places and who actually fell in love with me. A nice Jewish girl, it turned out. Grandmother favored the pair and later the four of us with a really nice allowance, although I was employed as an editor in a well established publishing house, cursive finally flattened out to texting.

Grandmother made one more trip across the pond to supervise what really needed no supervision in the by now ancestral manse. Grandmother Bubba lived on her memories and my visits for many more years.

*Doolally Tap: a small town in Western India, the formert site of a British Army transit camp where soldiersd were sent to recuperate if they were considered a bit nuts, crazy, bonkers. A rehabilitation station.

THE MISSION

'Twas a stark and dormi night that sleepy <u>32 Decree</u> **Master Meson** <u>Knight of the Order of the Quark</u> Sir Ichbin Ayyid, rode out of the Universal Rescue Center Headquarters^ on a mision. He prefers to be known as **MM** henceforward, it taking too long a time before entering into combat to recite his full designation whether he was challenging a dragon or an IRS agent.

MM Ichbin was scheduled to rescue the reclusive Princess Shikselah from some as yet undetermined peril. He did think of himself as the Paladin, the White Knight on a white steed. It helped sometimes on his missions and quests: it was a tremendous morale builder, if not exactly correct.

Undetermined peril, because the URC also professed to predict the future by means of wild guesses and statistics. Wild guesses proved right 55% of the time. This gave the URC an undeserved reputation of being correct in its assessment of situations 99.9% of the time. The .01% was wiggle room. The mission also remained undetermined because no one at URC could find the statistical and indetermination tables relating to the rescue of reclusive princesses.

Another factor was that the strands of the world wide web of URC vibrated when the key words "princess", "tower" and "reclusive" vibrated into URCHQ. A name was randomly plucked from a dedicated list of qualified rescuers. MM's name came up and thus it happened that:

MM spurred his steed Schlepper through the stark and dormi night onward toward the Kingdom of Schwartzyur as night and MM jogged toward day to what he hoped was a safe resolution of the undetermined peril.

MM trotted alongside of Schlepper toward his goal, not wanting to tire the equine over much until the need was felt for action. They halted occasionally for a refreshing pit stop, whether or not there was a pitstopping inn at hand.

MM was a stalwart lad of undistinguished features, average age, height, weight and fingerprints, undistinguishable in a crowd of other MMs, ordinary serfs, peasants, esnes, laborers, even the highborn* aristocracy or the common folk. That's probably why he was chosen to represent URC on missions of undetermined peril, random plucking not being what it once was.

MM fancied himself more of a lover than a mounted warrior. The word "Princess" might have ignited a spark within him and spurred him onward missionward.

As he neared the Kingdom of Schwartzyur, he could not help but ponder upon his mission. He couldn't call it a "quest" because a he wasn't questing for anything, except perhaps a winsome lass encountered somewhere in his missioning.

Women were attracted to MM because of his ability to be nearly invisible in a crowd. They may have seen him as a desirable will-o-the-wisp, just beyond their touch. MM visibly touched some of them, so there may be clones of MM here and there.

MM approached the border of Schwartzyur in good spirits, method-acting as an unemployed Samurai in search of a patron, thus passing over the border with appropriate humility and humbleness under the gaze of the slightly contemptuous border guards. Too many unemployed Samurai. That's another story.

He consulted his pocket Atlas and GPS as to the location of the royal hangout, not trusting to ask for directions, since he was afraid that his foreign accounts would betray him. He need not have worried, since he was a master of dialects and languages. But he was caution personified, confident of his abilities and at the same time lacking a modicum of self confidence; a conflicted lad, who often argued with himself. He was never sure who won.

There it was! The royal hang out! Standard crenellated towers and all! Now to discreetly locate the place where the Princess was supposed to be held against her will. Sometimes, MM came across Princeseses holding their Wills.

A tower apart from the rest of the royal hangout captured MM's attention as a likely place for the Princess to be holed up in at within.

Windows spiraled around the tower. The last was illuminated, silhouetting a shadow. The profile left no doubt as to the gender of the shadow.

MM exulted! This must be the place! Now to communicate with the tower's inhabitant as to the psychical specifics of her situation so that he may act accordingly and psychologically.

MM considered how to communicate. The most efficient way, he concluded, was to fasten a note to a specially constructed arrow and aim it to a point near the window frame rather than aim directly into the room, which might pierce the object of his mission, negating the whole situation.

How to alert Princess Shikselah as to incoming mail in a covert manner?

What he did was to trot near the tower, first ascertaining that there was a lack of sentries, guards, henchmen, sicarios or critters in the vicinity. It did not occur to him as to why there were no guardians around and about. He was to find out later why not.

He unlimbered his cow horn (as having a more soothing tone than a bull horn) from his saddle bag, positioning himself beneath the window and shouted in a penetrating whisper, "HEY, PRINCESS - INCOMING!"

Not anticipating a speedy reply because it was a cold call, he extracted his bow and arrow from his shoulder holster, unfolded it to its imposing length and width; This was a Foldable Message-Adaptable Archer's Delight, sold at most sporting good emporiums

He fastened a Form 436 Rescue-the-Princess letter, filling in her name, to the arrow, allowed for the added weight and windage, nocked the arrow, aimed and let fly. With a satisfying 'THUNK' it embedded itself in the window frame.

The Princess heard the shout and the subsequent 'THUNK'.

"Hmmm," she hmmmd. "I'm not expecting any mail. Must be a cold call. What the Hay, I'll check it out anyway. She reached out, extracted the arrow from the window frame and read the message. "It looks like a form letter. I see Form 436. Revised Djune in the Year of the Fuzzball in the lower left hand corner, filled out with my name and particulars inserted in beautiful handwriting in their proper spaces."

It read: *I hereby request that I be rescued from: kidnapers, lusters after my charms, fire, flood, earthquake, famine, the pox, heavy breathers, - Please fill in OTHERS. Please print legibly, keep the carbon copy, and hand the original to your rescuer, both of you arranging a rendezvous as soon as practicable.*

In the event that you do not wish to be rescued, disregard this letter, please notify your erstwhile rescuer by return arrow and move forward."

It was impressed **'MM. Ichbin Ayyid, 32 Decree Meson, Knight of the Order of the Quark and several other titles I am too modest to append to this seal.'** and initialed **MM.**

"Gosh Darn it, now my curiousity has been agitated. I'm going to follow this up," She stated.

Princess Shikselah was like unto a fairy tale Princess with slight modifications. She was six feet tall, a hazel eyed brunette of most shapely form and features. Her height enabled her to look down metaphorically and physically upon her would be suitors. She was of an age where her hormones sometimes but not quite overcame her virginmones.

Princess Shikselah was blissfully unaware of any mission concerning her rescue or any other disposition of herself. She was living a relatively happy existence at her daddy's court, repelling 99% percent of the courtiers and their varying states of lust. The other 1% enjoyed a modicum of snogging with hopes of further involvement in future. She was technically a virgin, thus entitled to be the object of a mission. Not a quest.

So the arrival of an arrowgram was unexpected.

She agreed that she wished to be rescued, keeping her fingers crossed, attached the completed form to the pouch affixed to the arrow and aimed it out of the window, shouting "FORE" softly, but loudly enough to disturb the bats in the belfry nearby.

MM saw the arrow gravitating toward him and ducked. It missed him and stuck in the saddle between his legs, which cause both horse and rider to emit emissions.

He read the completed form and he and Schlepper trotted around the tower and discovered a door. MM Ichbin pressed the button, saw the green light and announced. "It is I", and gave his full title and pedigree.

"Cut the BS and come on up, you pompous ass." was the reply.

Hurt, but unphased by the putdown, MM hurried up the circular stairs, puffing before he had reached the fifth floor, pausing for a moment to wish he had stayed on Schlepper.

"Hurry up before I lose interest," came a voice from a

centrally located speaker. "Good thing that you left the horse outside."

He hastily inhaled a deep breath and surged onward and upward, hoping the effort was worthwhile.

Finally, he reached the topmost landing and knocked on the portal.

"It's open. Come on in."

He did so, almost collapsing on the rug. As he struggled to keep his balance, he noticed a small sign next to a discreetly camouflaged door. 'Elevator" it read.

The Princess noticed his noticing the notice and chortled, "Gotcha, MM!"

"Some way to start a rescue," MM thought. He then focused on the Princess. "Holy Messiah-to-Come! A Babe of Babes!"

So with mixed emotions he found a seat, sank into it and started his customary spiel. Before he could get out the first syllable, she spoke unto him,

"OK, MM, what's your game? Tell me true, now, or I'll dis-organ you and toss your remains out the window for the voracious Chowhounds below. I am a Ebony Belt in MegaMagaBustYerButt and several other self-defense and agressive martial arts."

MM gulped and revised his spiel. "Fair Princess, I have come to rescue from the various and sundry situations mentioned in my communicative arrowgram. I...."

"I don't need to be rescued, I just wanna know what your game is. I'm tired of His Royal Pain in the Ass my father the King bugging me to tie the knot, The only knots I tied were the in the various appendages of the punters who my Dad invited to Court. One of those disgruntled punters let slip that I was adopted, when I spurned his advances and twisted his appendages.

That caught my attention. The twisted one whipped out a document and sneeringly handed it to me. I read and believed it. Maybe I was a royal blow-by. Maybe I was this or that. Don't know and don't care. I am happy here.

"I must say, your arrowgram was a novel approach."

This frankness was refreshing to MM. "Please explain your adoption if you want to. I much appreciate your candour. May I speak now?"

She acquiesed and MM spoke unto her and explained that he had been sent on a mission to the Kingdom of Schwartzyur to rescue the Princess of the Kingdom from an unspecified danger.

"I'm being candid in telling you this because you are a stranger and because I am bored out of my skull. I found out from my nanny, who has since spiraled up to Prime Nannyhood in the sky that I was left on the royal kitchen doorstep as an infant a couple of decades ago. Nanny happened to be entertaining the greengrocer at the time and answered the knock at the door. She paused in her entertainment and attended to the knock. There I was, such a bonny babe that nanny took me to her bosom immediately and dismissing the greengrocer.

She later introduced me to the King, who was enthralled by my bonnyness and raised me as his daughter, being childless at the time. The Queen, Rosaputin, usually agreed with the King and had nothing much to say about the abandoned baby. Another mouth to feed didn't mean much in the Royal Household, what with full grainaries. The royal couple did have some offspring later on, who promptly sprang off to various parts. I was no obstacle to their inheritance. They were not jealous of me because I was a mere female, and illegitimate, at that.

As I came of age, the King wished to marry me off,

considering what happened the courtiers and gropers as I detailed above and wishing no lawsuits or kerfuffles."

I am not locked up in this tower against my will. I took up residence here, with all creature comforts provided, to get away from gropers and sundry perverts. I can dis-lodge myself if I want to. So far, I am lodged comfortably, thank you." Shikselah reclined into a bean bag.

King RasPutin was a father figure to his subjects, and a real father to many others of his subjects. That is at least one reason why he let Princess Shikselah do much as she pleased; no unexpected pregnancies, please. Not a case of like father, like daughter.

MM was paralyzed with enchantment, his eyes focussed upin the bow-shaped, delicious lips of the bonny speaker. She stared back at him in sudden awareness of something.

"Say, when you look at me like that, you sort of look like me around the ears... Where do you hail from, otherwise indistinguishable as you are?"

The Knight gulped and stared at the Princesses ears, shapely as they were, with a small dark spot on each lobe. He had the same marks on his lugs.

Coincidence? Could she, was she, no, it couldn't be, never in a million years.... but wait! Wasn't one of his contacts, as he liked to call them, a winsome lass, taller than he was - vertically but not horizontally, of the same lobish configuration as his present company?

And, Princess Shikselah was adopted! Oy Vey! Was he lusting after his own daughter? He did remember that that winsome lass of long ago confided in him that she was gravid and there was no one else but him who 'knew' her. He tended to believe her. So he did a midnight flit.

MM always intended to do right by her after overcoming his midnight flit emotions, but events and missions, plus a rather disasterous quest, made that not feasible. What goes around, comes around. Now, he just couldn't wait for any not-so-fool-poof DNA nonsense. He had a gut feeling about this andd he went with his gut.

The Princess hung a "DO NOT DISTURB, LEAVE ALL COMMUNICATIONS AND FOOD BY THE ELEVATOR DOOR" sign on the front door knob. MM used the elevator, slapped Schlepper on the rump and told him to go home and wait for him.

Shikselah and Ichbin spent the night and several days exploring the circumstance of their lives, suppositions and other happenings. They concluded that they were indeed father and daughter and composed a letter to King RasPutin detailing the whole saga.

The couple sent the missive by way of the Archer's Arrow, thunking it in the window frame of the King's study. Startled, the King retrieved the letter. After several time periods of contemplation, he sighed, wrote a brief "goodbye and good luck" reply, attached a few gold coins to the arrow pouch and sent it by courier to the tower.

MM and Shikselah rejoiced and made plans.

Could this mean that he could quit quests and missions and retire? Let Schlepper out to pasture and buy a farm horse and cultivate that farm he had bought when he had a peso or two and almost forgotten about it.

Shikselah was carried off, if not married off, not by royalty but by a respected, average person who happened to be her biological father. It did decrease to zero the number of courtiers from various other regions from bothering the King and suing the Kingdom of Schwartzyur for damages of their twisted appendages.

MM and Shikselah ambled off into the sunset. MM became plain Ichbin Ayyid, renouncing all titles, but enjoying a modest pension, whilst Shikselah rejoyced in her new found father and found, after a fruitful search, a six foot five former Foosball player who done good by her.

Ichbin is now a respected farmer who raises kumquats and enjoys his numerous grandkids. He also, much to his surprise, married the mother of his daughter, confering a "post-legitimacy" upon Shikselah and thought about siblings for her.

Incidentally. this entire report has been recently declared "UNCLASSIFIED" by the URC.

Who says there's no such thing as "they existed happily ever after"

The end, possibly. One does not leave the URC so easily. We shall see.

Scripsit 436

*highborn because they were taller than the rest of the above mentioned. MM Ichbin sometimes chose to wear elevator shoes on certain assignments.

^The RCU is a for-profit-when-they-can-get-it organization operating on various time-lines which rescues entities, sentient or not, sometimes whether they do not want or need rescuing. Whilst operating out of Central Headquarters Nexus, each franchise owner is allowed a certain latitude in his/hers/its/$#@/ dimension or sphere of influence. They/*^&%/ do submit quarterly reports to CHN and are chided or commended accordingly as to their actions and they receive news of the other franchises. They do co-operate and sometimes have friendly competitions as to the the number of missions and quests successfully accomplished. MM actually won several trophies!

> Lower Middle Bronix.

Printed in the United States
By Bookmasters